THE UNDERWOOD SEE

ORCHARD BOOKS
338 Euston Road, London NW1 3BH
Orchard Books Australia
Level 17/207 Kent Street, Sydney, NSW 2000

ISBN: 978 1 84121 170 1

First published in 2006 by Orchard Books
First published in paperback in 2007
Text © Michael Lawrence 2006

A CIP catalogue record for this book is available from the British Library.

1 3 5 7 9 10 8 6 4 2

Printed in Great Britain

Orchard Books is a division of Hachette Children's Books,
an Hachette Livre UK company

MICHAEL LAWRENCE

THE UNDERWOOD SEE

BOOK THREE OF
THE ALDOUS LEXICON

ORCHARD BOOKS

For I.E. and M.A.S, my parents,
who, by randomly introducing
a particular sperm to a particular ovum,
created (hopefully with pleasure)
the eventual author of this trilogy,
which is set in the very house
in which the coupling took place.

AUTHOR'S NOTE

The Aldous Lexicon is a single story in three volumes. A reading in chronological order is recommended to avoid confusion, that order being: A CRACK IN THE LINE, SMALL ETERNITIES, THE UNDERWOOD SEE.

The house known as Withern Rise stands a little to one side of a substantial parcel of land which the founder divided for ease of reference into four parts. Thus we have the north, south and east gardens, but no west garden as such, this being the grassy strip that slopes down to the river from the original front of the house, now very much the back. This part of the garden is casually referred to as 'the river side'.

There are two magnificent weeping willows in the grounds, one in the north garden, the other near the southern end of the landing stage, abutting a corner of the south garden. Aldous Underwood lives beneath the second of these in Naia's present reality, but it is the willow in the north garden that is the focus of much of the activity in this volume.

There are things known and there are things unknown, and in between are the doors of perception...
Aldous Huxley, 1954

If something occurs outside what we call the natural order, its very smallness may be more immediately unnerving than, for instance, the eclipse of the sun to a tribe without astronomy, where holy awe must over-ride any other feeling. Very small cracks in our outer shell of reason let in very cold air.
Lucy M. Boston: Memory in a House, 1973

Everything happens for a reason — *Anon*
Horse manure — *Aldous U.*

CONTENTS

FLASH 1

Naia was thirty-one and driving home to revive a lapsed tradition: to give birth to an Underwood at Withern Rise. October night. Rain hammering the windscreen. Her curses for the dark, the weather, everything, everything. So much to curse these days. Where had it all gone wrong? When? So many split seconds when her life might have spun in a different direction; probably had, elsewhere, over and over again. She'd long since got out of the habit of trying to pinpoint those critical instants when her future swung in the balance. Better that way. Saner. You couldn't change much in the reality you were stuck with.

The rhythm of the sluggish wipers carving gleaming fragments of roadway scrambled her thoughts, returned her to that other October fourteen years earlier, when the second major upheaval of her life had occurred. Those fateful few days. The days of two more Alarics, the man who called himself Aldous U, and the multiple realities of the Underwood See...

Part One

PERIPHERAL VISIONS

1: 39

Sometimes there were whispers in the night, and no one there when she opened her eyes or looked round corners. She'd stopped believing in ghosts when she was ten, and at seventeen considered the very idea of them absurd, so, even with her very uncommon awareness of the way things were, she tried to shrug off such incidents as the products of an over-developed imagination. But even she was spooked by the business of the tap.

She'd woken early, crawled out of bed after a lingering embrace with the duvet, and, shivering because the heating wasn't yet on, padded barefoot to the window overlooking the river. Condensation blurred the view. She cut a swathe with the edge of her hand. So still out there. State of pause before the world came alive. She tugged her dressing gown on and, after a visit to the bathroom, headed downstairs. A bundle of white fur was waiting for her on the halfway platform. 'Can't bear to be alone, can you?' she said, stepping over it. The little creature followed her down, step for step, trying to keep pace. It still wore the tag around its neck, but since June she'd found it hard to use the name she'd assigned to it. It had been fine as long as she thought she'd never see Alaric again, but then she had seen him, and afterwards it felt wrong to address the cat by his name. Mostly, now, she simply called it 'Cat'.

Next stop, the kitchen. And that was when it happened. She was about to fill the kettle when the handle of the tap turned of its own accord. Water spurted. She jumped back. The tap continued to run for about seven seconds, then turned itself off. She put the kettle down and left the room. The cat followed her across the hall.

In the Long Room, she drew the curtains back from the French windows and leant there, trying not to think about the self-turning tap. She already had a theory about it, but did her utmost to put it from her. She was trying to be *normal*, for God's sake. Normal people didn't have ideas like that. She picked the cat up, cradled it the way it liked, and encouraged her mind to wander. It wandered with her gaze to the willow over to the right of the windows. Aldous was asleep in there, within that great inverted bowl of leaves. She worried about Aldous. Tried not to let it show when he was around, but she did worry. There was ground-frost some mornings now. The days were getting cooler. At the weekend the clocks would go back. Shorter days, longer nights: much colder nights soon. It was bad enough already, the nights he spent in there, his only light a lamp they'd rigged up for him, but how would he fare in the dead of winter, when the leaves were gone? He'd be so *exposed*.

She thought back to the day Aldous moved to the willow from his leafy enclosure across the river. She'd hoped to persuade him to take one of the spare rooms, but he'd refused point-blank. Couldn't bear to be indoors for any length of time, he said. He'd tried to fix up his manky old hammock, but the boughs of the willow weren't right, so she and Kate had bought him a padded sleeping bag from the sports shop in town and a camp bed from the Army and Navy store. They would have kitted him out more comfortably, but she'd doubted he would take any but the humblest of offerings, and she was right. He accepted the bed with a sniff of disdain, but was suspicious of the pristine blue bag.

'Brand new.'

'I bought it a while back to go camping with friends,' she lied.

'Never been used.'

'The trip fell through.'

'Well it's yours, not mine.'

'I don't mind you using it.'

'You might need it.'

'I won't. I don't have any more camping plans.' When he still hesitated, she said: 'If you don't take it I'll give it to a charity shop, where someone will buy it for next to nothing. If you have it, it'll at least get some use and I won't feel my money's been wasted.'

'Well...' he said slowly, and so it became his, as a personal favour.

At first the night shufflings of the ranks of stemlike branches had kept Aldous awake, but he'd got used to that. He was back in the garden where his mind told him he'd played so recently, right by the house he was born in, and up there the window of his old room, Naia's room now. He was just grateful to be there after so long away.

He still went walking around and beyond Eynesford and Stone most days, but he hadn't crossed into any of his 'other lives' since taking up residence under the willow. This did not dismay him, but it puzzled him. Was it because he was back where he belonged? Because he knew who he was again? He wished he could talk to someone about these things, but he feared people would think he was off his chump. Even Naia might think that. Even Mr Knight. If he'd still been able to visit the other lives he might have told the Mr Knight who lived in one of them, but he daren't risk it now with only one of him. He was glad there was a Mr Knight here. Glad he helped in the garden. He enjoyed their chats, and sometimes they shared a pot of tea made from water boiled on the little camp stove Naia and Kate had made him take. He liked Naia and Kate too, but he wished they wouldn't keep giving him things. Made him feel beholden. Maman always said that presents were only for special occasions. Maman had been suspicious of presents that came at other times. She was even suspicious of flowers from Father, but Father had given them anyway. Quite often. Beautiful flowers. He missed Father. Missed him terribly.

2: 36

Four months after the event, Alex was far from over Alaric's death. Whenever she stood by the river she saw the body they'd pulled out in June. Wherever she went in the garden or the house, he was there. She could hardly bear to enter his room. His now silent, unchanging room. To remain at Withern, where she believed he'd passed all of his seventeen years, would be a never-ending torment for her. There was nothing of him here now but memories, not even a grave; they'd scattered his ashes on the water from the landing stage. When she told Ivan of her wish to move away, he did not protest. His loss was greater than any he'd ever experienced, but for him there was something more: regret that he hadn't, as he remembered it, shown his son more than passing affection for the better part of half-a-dozen years. There was shame, too, that he would be the one to sell the house built by an Underwood; the house which, apart from a sixteen year interlude way back, had been in the family for over a hundred and twenty years. If they moved away – as they must – he would also have to sell the business. The years he'd put in at that shop, struggling to make it pay! In the weeks and months following Alaric's death, he had continued to go in six days a week, and on Sundays wished he was there. The shop was his refuge from the oppressive silence that now permeated every part of Withern Rise.

Unlike her husband, Alex had nowhere to hide and few distractions. For one of the few times in her life she hadn't a creative thought in her head. Half-term didn't help. No College, no animated chats with her students. Apart from shopkeepers and the odd friend who popped in, the only person she saw was Mr Knight, and he was only there part-time. Until the tragedy she'd often pottered outside with him. They hadn't spoken much while they worked, but she found him comfortable to be around. He'd carried on working in the garden after Alaric's death, a day here, half a day there, and some weeks had passed before she realised that she hadn't paid him in all that time. Appalled, she'd rushed out to apologise.

'Oh, haven't you?' he said, as if it were news to him.

'You know I haven't. Why didn't you remind me?'

'Because it's not important, Alex. I can manage.'

'That's not the point. We made an agreement and I haven't honoured it. Look, I haven't much cash in the house. Can I write you a cheque?'

'You can write it,' he said.

Picking up on the subtext – 'But I'll not cash it' – which she put down to pity, she said: 'I'll have the cash for next time.' But it was curious. After that brief conversation about money they were friends, where previously they'd merely been acquaintances with a garden in common. When she next saw him, a couple of days later, she handed him the overdue wages and he pocketed the notes with ill-concealed embarrassment. From that day on she invited him in more often than before, for elevenses, a bread-and-cheese lunch, a cup of fruit tea in the afternoon, and he would linger, not saying much, but comforting her with his solid, uncomplicated presence.

It was because of her liking and respect for Mr Knight that she had shown him the peculiar letter she'd found under Alaric's bed after his death. An odd thing, not really a letter at all, signed 'Aldous U, Withern Rise', which she could make no sense of. He had read the typed pages carefully, but when he finished could offer no explanation for it other than 'Something some imaginative chum cooked up?', a possibility she had no desire to investigate but which covered the matter and allowed her to file it away, in its crude envelope, with her late son's other effects.

Mr Knight had also been there the day she and Ivan had agreed to put the house on the market. His expression on hearing the news had come across as a mixture of interest and dismay.

'Where will you go?'

'We haven't decided. We're not tied to anywhere. If we sell we'll be quite well off for a change.'

'Yes. Property this size, right by the river. But your purchaser might not have the feeling you do for it.'

Alex shrugged. 'We can't impose our wishes on future owners.'

'So it'll come down to money. The best offer.'

'Isn't that the way it usually works?'

'I believe so. Usually.'

This seemed to sadden him rather.

3: 39

When Naia started along the path from the side gate on returning from an errand in the village, she saw Mr Knight raking dead leaves into heaps over in the south garden, watched by Aldous sitting on the side of the old wheelbarrow. Cosy scene, rich in cliché: crisp pale sun in a clear blue sky, woodsmoke unspooling from a corner of the veggie patch, gardener raking leaves watched by an old chap on a wheelbarrow, and, in an upstairs window, Kate polishing glass with a yellow cloth. Times like this she could forget that she didn't belong here; almost believe that the life she'd lived until February was nothing more than an array of self-indulgent daydreams.

Mr Knight stopped work as she approached. 'Just the gal,' he said.

'Why, what's up?'

From a pocket of the faded check jacket he wore on all but the warmest days, he drew an envelope. A particular kind of envelope, hand-made, waterproof, the flap sealed with a blob of red wax impressed with the letter 'A'. Her name was written on the front, in capitals.

'Where did this come from?'

Mr Knight nodded towards the Family Tree. 'Sticking out of that.'

Aldous smirked. 'Love letter?'

'Some hopes.'

She stuffed the envelope in a back pocket and walked as casually as she could to the front door, which in her haste she opened too sharply, bumping Kate, tidying shoes on the other side of it. She muttered an apology but did not stop; hurried along the hall to the River Room, whose door she closed firmly behind her.

4: 47

Another Kate Faraday at another Withern Rise stood before that reality's Family Tree, in which no envelopes had ever been found. Not having climbed or played around this tree as a child she had no feeling for it other than admiration for the look of it. But the old oak was far less grand this autumn than in previous years. Its leaves were withered and brown where they should be robust and golden. The ground was littered with these sorry specimens, curling on the lawn like small arthritic hands. Kate and Ivan had called experts in, heard the verdict, and were debating what to do for the best. If left standing, the tree could become brittle and unsafe, but if they removed it this part of the garden would be nothing but an expanse of flat grass whose one passably interesting feature was the strip of wild wood – traditionally ignored – along the southern boundary wall.

'Problem?'

She turned. 'I was wondering what we should do about this old thing.'

'And?'

'We may not have much choice. Would you mind very much?'

Alaric shrugged. 'It's just a tree.'

She suspected that it was more than just a tree to him, but let it go – he never gave much in conversation – and considered the garden as a whole. She'd toiled here for hours on end through the summer, but it was a battle just to keep it tidy. Her expertise in Victorian furniture and early twentieth century collectables did not qualify her for the role of head gardener at Withern Rise.

'We could do with help here. Too much for us alone.' Too much for her, she meant. With a sigh, and a bleak 'Oh, well,' she returned to the house.

Alaric watched her go, deflated. He'd approached her at the tree with the intention of getting some sort of dialogue going, and as usual hadn't even got started. He'd lost count of the times he'd tried to tell her that he was pleased she was with them and ended up mumbling something else entirely. What must she think of him? Typical seventeen-year-old, morose, monosyllabic, resentful of all he surveyed and anyone older than himself? It wasn't that Kate was hard to talk to. Not at all. She was warm, open, encouraging. It was him. No idea how to express himself, say what he felt. He wanted to be able to chat with her about trivial things, laugh at silly observations or something on the telly, like he used to with Mum. Above all he wanted to make her feel welcome. But he couldn't manage it. She'd been here eight months, and he hadn't come close.

From Kate and his failure, Alaric turned to the tree from which he'd kept his distance for most of the year. The memory of what happened when he touched it that night in February still disturbed his sleep on occasion. It was just two weeks since he'd finally found the nerve to approach it again, reasoning that although

26

it might send him to a Withern Rise in which a terrible deed had taken place, it might, just as easily, send him to Naia's. He had placed his hands on the trunk, as he had that other time, but nothing had happened. Nothing at all. There wasn't even a hint that anything *could* happen. He had done this several times since that day, always with the same result, forcing the conclusion that whatever power the tree had possessed in February was not present in October. There might be a good reason for this, of course. In February it had not been dying.

From the old oak he drifted round the southern side of the house, and down the steps to the landing stage. He seated himself cross-legged on the bare boards and gazed at the water. So still here. The only movement a swarm of tiny insects circling nothing visible to the human eye. Only sound the water easing by. Most peaceful place he knew when there were no boats passing. When he was younger he used to jump in from here, splash about, swim back and forth between the banks. Mum had always insisted that he keep within the bounds of the landing stage, where it was known to be quite shallow, but occasionally – this would have horrified her if she'd known about it – he'd crouched down there on the river bed to see how long he could go without air. That last-minute surge to the surface, that first huge gulp of breath, had been so exhilarating. He smiled at the memory. The things you do when you're a kid. But he imagined going just that bit further now that he was older; staying under past the point of safe return, floating to the surface, lungs full of water, to be found, mourned, remembered tenderly forever.

As he sat contemplating death, glory and other inconsequentials, a feeling crept over him like a shadow, and he looked up to a world less tangible than before. He was instantly alert. Twisting round to take in what he could of the garden from there, he saw many duplications of it, each one slightly out of phase with its neighbours. More fascinated than alarmed, it seemed to him at first that each version was identical, but then he noticed tiny differences: some leaves cut back, a shrub in one but not the others, the same birds in the sky but in slightly altered formations.

He got up, slowly, hardly daring to blink for fear of losing all this. He faced the house. The walls were hazily transparent, and within them stood a much smaller building that looked as though it had been assembled in haste from a heap of clumsily-sliced boulders. He heard voices to his left, and turned his head. A group of boys, mooching. A little less distinct than they would be if actually present, they seemed unaware of him – until one of them glanced his way and stopped as if he'd hit a wall; stared back at him in astonishment as he and his pals, along with the peculiar building and the multiple views, faded away.

5:39

In the River Room, Naia broke the seal of the envelope and drew out a sheet of paper on which a message had been typed with a manual typewriter that would have benefited from a change of ribbon. She knew who it must be from, but nevertheless checked the name of the sender, also typed, at the foot of the page. Back in June, when she found the second missive from this person, she was convinced that Aldous had written them – same name, after all – but her first real conversation with him had eliminated him as a suspect. As there'd been no others she'd tried to forget about the letters, stop wondering who'd put them in the tree, but here was a third, four months on, and she could not ignore it. She sat down on the old chaise-longue to read the following:

    Naia, I'm writing this because there are things I wish to speak to you about – in person, here in my adopted reality.

To save time when we meet, let me tell you, very briefly, how all this began.

Like you, I was sixteen when I learnt that mine was not the only reality. Like you, I discovered this truth at Withern Rise. I was in the garden when I came across a way through, though the reality I found myself in was so like my own that I didn't realise I was in another until a stranger demanded to know what I was doing there. He was an Underwood, and he lived there. There were no Underwoods at the Withern I knew.

Following that first experience I found I could visit many realities from the same point. I'll tell you about some of those early outings when we meet. About them and very much more. Look in the tree just before mid-day tomorrow for instructions as to how to get to me.

Aldous U.

Withern Rise

She was about to read the letter again when she heard a footfall outside. She went to the door, looked out, and saw a figure walking away from her along the hall.

She gave an involuntary cry, but the other Naia did not stop, or even glance back. She was almost at the front door when she vanished.

6: 114/43

Ric hadn't told the others what he'd seen. A boy who looked like him – the way he used to look – and the house he'd grown up in. He'd only glimpsed them, then it was just these trees again, but he'd seen them all right. He wished he had an explanation for them, but explanations were hard to come by these days. Nothing had made sense since he came here – wherever 'here' was.

The day it happened, a warm Sunday afternoon in July, he'd been in the north garden, sitting against the trunk of the willow (so reminiscent of old elephant hide), sifting through the latest prints of Garth Noy and Bonnie Barraco getting it on. Noy had a nice little business going there, and an enthusiastic partner in Bonnie the Bike. The things that girl would do for the camera! When he heard a scuffling behind him, the pictures flew and he jumped guiltily to his feet and darted round the trunk. Relieved to find no one there, he took a further step, intending to complete the circuit and return to the snaps. The step was half-completed when he experienced a rush of something very like dizziness and the willow was replaced by a great many more trees, all crowding in on him, and a far from pleasant odour. Alarmed, he rushed this way and that, and in so doing quickly lost all sense of his point of arrival. There was nothing but trees in every direction, so densely packed and leafed that little light filtered between or through them. He found no paths as such, merely suggestions of a few that petered out at once, and the two short flights of worn steps he came across climbed only to empty space.

After a time he forced himself to pause, calm down. What this place was and how he got here could be worked out later. For now he must be less headstrong, more methodical in his search either for a way out or a way back, whichever came first. But even proceeding with more circumspection he was unsuccessful. There seemed to be no end to these woods; no splinter of full daylight anywhere he looked or went. He wandered all afternoon and evening, with mounting hopelessness, and passed the night curled up in a leafy bower, shivering, not with cold but with fear; fear that he was lost forever, that he would never again see the world and people he knew.

In the morning – how early he couldn't say, having tripped over a root and smashed his watch the night before – he continued his search. Hours passed, futile hours, and eventually, very hungry and thirsty, he sank to the ground in despair.

'Who the feckin' hell are you?'

A heavy-set youth with an unruly mop of ginger hair had stepped out of the bushes.

'I...'

The attempt was dismissed with a wave of the hand. 'Who cares? Company's company.'

The boy gave his name as Scarry, but misheard the one offered in return, picking up on the last syllable only, an abbreviation which went uncorrected then and in the months that followed.

'What is this place?' the newly-named Ric had asked.

Scarry snorted. 'Whatcha think it is? Buncha feckin' trees that go on forever, that's what it is.'

'It must end somewhere.'

'If it does, it ain't nowhere near here. I been here weeks and never seen nothing but feckin' trees.'

What Scarry did not mention was that he'd spent a great many days during those lonely, frightened weeks desperately seeking a way out, and that this tangled, festering forest had frustrated him at every turn. To tell of this would have been to admit failure to someone who didn't know that he'd never succeeded in a damn thing he'd ever tried.

'Wanna see my house?' he asked brightly.

'Your house?'

'Yeah. This way.'

Scarry's house turned out to be three ruined ivy-laden walls that met to form two corners of a primitive dwelling that had tumbled to its foundations an age ago. These remnant walls, no more than a yard-and-a-half at their highest, partially enclosed a bed of rock so irregular that it might have risen in a single convulsion aeons since – may even have caused the collapse. The remainder of the building had devolved into a contiguous scatter of rocky hummocks overrun with vines, and knolls thick with moss and lichen. There might once have been a door and windows, but there was no sign of them now, while the ceiling was a tangled lattice of branches and leaves that stretched from the middle reaches of the trees that stood like sentries all about. Scarry said that the one time it had rained since he'd been there the trees had provided perfect shelter.

'Must get cold at night, though,' Ric said.

'Not so much. Not so far.'

He was proud of his residence. It was the first home he'd had where no one lorded it over him, told him what to do, sneered at him.

'Is there anyone else here?'

'Only the old geezer,' Scarry said. 'I keep my distance from him.'

'Old geezer?'

'First time I saw him, he yelled at me. Typical. They always yell. My foster folks yelled at me all the time. Threw stuff, cracked me round the head. Frank raised his feckin' fist whenever I walked in. And the probation officer, Griffiths, talked to me like I was scum. The old geezer's the same. Knew it the minute I saw him. Keep away from him, that's an order.'

It was Scarry's first order, and it established their relative positions here. Ric didn't care about position. He was grateful for the food his new friend shared with him – some potato-like vegetables he'd baked overnight in the embers of a fire – and the clear water he showed him, running over rocks nearby.

A few days after Ric's arrival, the first of the others turned up – young Jonno – and, a couple of days after him, Hag and Badger, together. Jonno was twelve, the eldest of the three. He said that he and his pal Hendrix had climbed over the wall of this old house one night, for a nose around. He'd hidden under this big tree to freak Hendrix out, and next thing he knew he was in these whiffy woods, alone, and he panicked and just ran and ran. When he finally stopped and shouted his mate's name, Scarry and Ric came along.

Hag and Badger – Scarry too – had also been near a tree in some garden moments before they walked into the forest. None of them named the species of tree or the property in whose grounds it stood, but from what they said Ric knew that, like him, they'd come here from the willow in the north garden of Withern Rise. While the three younger boys had climbed the wall or crept along the drive with mere mischief in mind, Scarry was pleased to relate that he'd planned to break into the house and swipe something from the 'rich shits' who lived there. The only one who hadn't been trespassing was Ric, but he kept this to himself.

As the second to arrive, and the nearest to Scarry's age, he was the one the head man talked to the most. The others were just 'the kids', whose role, as subordinates, was to do as they were told, which for the most part meant gathering wood, lighting the fires, and cooking what little flesh that could be caught or found. The kids missed home dreadfully. Home, parents, their beds, proper food and drink. They sniffled and cried quite a bit at first, until Scarry made a rule: 'No more whingeing 'bout where you feckin' come from – right? No more lost this, lost that. You're here, this is it, feckin' put up with it, 'kay?'

But not talking about these things didn't stop the longing, the misery. The only difference was that suffering was now conducted in silence, or alone while drifting hopelessly about the forest. And it wasn't only the young boys who suffered. Ric did too. More than he could say. More than he was allowed to.

7: 114

In his time, the man who signed himself Aldous U (known simply as 'AU' to a few acquaintances) had come across several incarnations of himself, none of whom had turned out like him, *all* of whom he went out of his way to avoid. In some realities he was a landscape gardener, in others a hotel manager. In a couple he was a painter-and-decorator who ran an Internet porn site on the side. In one he was a comic-book writer and illustrator who'd sold the rights to his series about dark invaders to an independent film-maker named Bobby Rodriguez. Discovering that he was a man of the cloth in another, he was sorely tempted to spin him round and slap him for being so naïve. (He didn't; merely made a swift head-shaking exit.)

But it wasn't only versions of himself he kept away from. To avoid confusion he steered clear of people he'd conversed with at length in other realities. One of the few recent exceptions to this had been Naia's garden guest, an Aldous very different to himself in all respects but name. They'd first met in January when this old man strolled out of thin air a few yards from where he was standing, and continued walking without missing a step as if he'd been on that path all along. Fascinated by such an extraordinary ability, AU had befriended Aldous, and, when he located the reality from which he'd emerged, befriended him in that one too, as another version of himself. In both realities, as they got to know one another, Aldous had spoken of the misfortune that had turned him into an old man while he slept. Although compelled to listen to the same tale twice with trivial variations, in the months that followed their first encounter AU, in his two identical personas, had tried to help his new friend adjust to the world and century into which he'd been catapulted. He did this because he felt a very great sympathy for him, but also because they shared a name, though this was another detail he kept to himself. It was a puzzle to him that Aldous appeared in just one reality these days, but this too could not be discussed between them.

Of late, AU had cut back on visits to realities in which he was not known, largely because – his point of entry invariably being the grounds of a Withern Rise –

he was sick of being called to account by owners who spotted him, or pursued by a pair of yapping terriers or some larger beast. But now and then the old urge to experience the unfamiliar recurred, and off he would go. On one recent occasion he found himself at a Withern transformed into a retirement home, the grounds landscaped to accommodate neat islands of lawn dotted with benches, and careful paths for residents to be pushed along in wheelchairs. This was a fairly amusing variation, but some were far from amusing – like one visited a few weeks back.

The garden of the Withern Rise he entered that September afternoon had seemed very standard, if somewhat dishevelled. After popping a handful of grasses and leaves into the leather wallet attached to his belt, he slipped out by the side gate and headed up to the village. It was a practice of his to buy a paper on a first visit to a reality; you never knew what advertisement or tiny story peculiar to it you might find if you looked hard enough. He was about to enter the newsagent's when he noticed that the shop across the road, which sold bicycles in most realities, was a rather tatty second-hand furniture shop, with, over the broad main window, a shoddily-painted yellow and blue sign bearing the legend 'Used Emporium'. This was a difference he'd never encountered before.

He did not have to look hard for a reality-specific story that day. Every front page carried a variant of a single headline that could not have appeared in any other reality that he knew of. Fascinated, he bought *The Times* and a paper called *The Examiner*. Carrying them back along the lane, reading as he went, he seated himself on the cemetery steps to study the many pages devoted to the big story. Absorbed, he did not hear the approaching footsteps, but he couldn't miss or ignore the voice.

'Shocking, isn't it?'

He looked up. A slightly plumper Ivan Underwood than usual stood before him. An Ivan who dyed his hair a darker shade than suited him. He too carried a newspaper: a tabloid.

'It certainly is.' AU got up, dusting the seat of his pants. 'I was just starting on the who-dun-it theories.'

Ivan waggled his paper. 'Hot favourite in this one's Saddam. Could be right. Gore should have gone after him once he spiked Bin Laden at Tora Bora. Now it's up to Kerry to sort him out.'

'Kerry?'

'Just think. If not for that insurance fiasco just before the second term election, Kerry wouldn't have been drafted in as Vice and it'd be President Lieberman now. Think Kerry's got the balls for that sort of action?

I'm not so sure. Fancy a beer?'

Aldous U liked a cold beer on a warm day, but this was not one of those days and he wasn't really thirsty. However, a chance to learn more about the political situation here – and the owners of this Withern Rise – was too good to pass up. He accepted with thanks.

Ushered as a guest through the gate he'd crept out of like a criminal a short while ago, AU was able to inspect the property at his leisure as they strolled along the path. This part of the garden looked as if it hadn't been touched since early summer. There were thistles and long grass where flowers and vegetables should be; once-healthy plants were struggling or choked by weeds; gravel was unraked; litter delivered by the wind remained where it had fallen. As they approached the house he saw that the drive, where it opened out before the front door and the kitchen window, was badly in need of weeding, though a few green clumps in the old wheelbarrow parked beside a grubby white Volvo estate suggested that someone had decided to make an effort. He saw who that someone was when she came out as they were about to enter.

Of all the Alex Underwoods he'd seen or met, this one was by far the most dismal. She was pale and gaunt, and her mouth seemed a stranger to smiles, while her hair, longer than most Alexes', might not have been brushed or combed for a week. She had the look of a woman who had suffered some profound disappointment or personal loss. Passing them on the step without a word or glance, she returned to her weeding while Ivan led the way inside, to the kitchen, where he took two cans of Rooneys from the fridge. They sat at the table and talked about President Gore's assassination and the implications of it for America and the world. Most of this came from Ivan, of course, AU's knowledge of this reality being limited to a few minutes' examination of a couple of newspapers on the cemetery steps. The slant and vigour of his host's views surprised him. He'd never come across such a right-wing, reactionary Ivan Underwood.

Ivan was well into his second beer – AU had declined another – when his thoughts turned to a topic much closer to home, in the course of which he disclosed that the used furniture 'emporium' in the village was his. No *Underwood's Antiques & Memorabilia* in Stone High Street for this Ivan. The sorry tale he was so keen to share with a stranger that overcast September afternoon went as follows. One Sunday a couple of months earlier, shortly after lunch, their teenage son – Al – had left the house. He hadn't said where he was going, but that was normal for him

42

these days. When he wasn't back by eleven that night Ivan had phoned the homes of Al's friends, the ones he had names or numbers for anyway. None of them had seen him all day. They waited till morning before calling the police in case he turned up in the middle of the night. Searches were then carried out, around the grounds, across the river, in the village and town. A few pornographic photos found under the old willow in the north garden were a mystery, but no clue as to where he'd gone or what might have happened to him. Statements were taken from Ivan and Alex and anyone who knew their son or might have come into contact with him recently. A two-year-old holiday picture of him with his face half in shade appeared in the local papers. In spite of all these efforts to locate him there'd been no trace of the boy since that Sunday. No sign, no sound, not a word.

'The wife's not handling it well,' Ivan said, nodding towards the window. 'Blames me. We hadn't been getting on so well lately, me and Al. She thinks I must've been having a go at him and he walked out in protest. But it wasn't me. I didn't drive him away.'

What Ivan didn't bother to mention while relating all this (mainly because it wasn't important to him) was that during the official search of the grounds radio contact with a young policewoman had been lost and never resumed. It was common knowledge among this officer's colleagues that she wasn't happy in the job, or with her Taekwon-Do-instructor husband, and the assumption was made that she'd borrowed a leaf from the boy's book and legged it; taken that plane to Honolulu – as she'd so often threatened to do – to join an old schoolfriend who worked in a casino there. If Ivan had told him about the disappearance of the policewoman, AU would have asked him if she'd last been seen near the willow in the north garden. If the answer had been yes, he, if no one else, would have been almost certain that wherever she was it was not Honolulu. At least, not the Honolulu of that reality.

8: 47/78

Kate had been about to go to the village shop for a few things when Alaric offered to go for her. She was pleased, not because she didn't have to go after all, but because he had volunteered, without any prompting.

He was just setting off when he saw a tortoiseshell cat wending a wayward course towards the north garden. He wasn't a cat lover, but this was one he hadn't seen before, so he followed it. Reaching the big willow, whose bulging folds of slender leaves fanned across the lawn and garnished the water below the riverbank, the cat slipped inside. When he too entered that muted realm, the cat glanced coolly back at him as if to say, 'Follow me or don't follow me, your choice,' and strolled round the trunk, tail in the air. Again he went after it, but when he got to the other side the cat wasn't there. While peering up to see if it was climbing, he took a further step, came over giddy, and ended the step leaning against the gnarled old trunk. By the time the giddiness had passed his interest in the cat had also waned, but when he returned to the garden he felt unaccountably on edge. Following the path to the gate, he looked neither right nor left, or even ahead, only at the ground in front of his feet. This preoccupation with something he could not identify was no doubt the cause of his failure to notice that the gate at the end of the path was in greater need of repair than it ought to be, or that it took a harder tug than usual to close it behind him.

Hunching up the lane and past the primary school tucked into the corner, he turned left into Main Street. Entering the village shop a little way along he was startled by a sharp buzz rather than the undisciplined ringing of the bell always, until now, attached to the inside of the door. He was further surprised to see an unfamiliar face behind the counter. The only time either Mr or Mrs Paine wasn't at the till was during their annual holiday, the same two weeks every August. If they'd taken a few extra days off for once, Lenny hadn't mentioned it. Still. Whatever. This woman was obviously standing in for them or helping out. He passed along the three short aisles with a basket from the stack behind the door: new baskets, blue plastic, about time too; the old metal ones had sharp bits sticking out of them. In minutes he had everything on the list. He put the basket on the counter. The woman began running his purchases across the scanner.

'Good deed for the day?'

'Sorry?'

'Shopping for Mum.'

'Something like that.'

'Live in the village, do you?'

'Down the lane,' he said.

'The bungalows?'

'No.' He hesitated – what was it to her? – but when she seemed to expect more, added: 'The house by the river. Withern Rise.'

The woman's hand froze above the carrier bag she was packing for him. 'Stace never said nothing about no lodger.'

'Stace?'

She dropped the box of tea bags in. 'Mrs Curtis. She's been alone there for nine years, since…' She gave him a sharp, bright look. 'It's all right, you don't have to say where you live, just me being nosy.'

'No, I really live th…' He trailed off, suddenly in need of allies. 'Mr and Mrs Paine know me.'

'Who?'

Her expression suggested that she'd never heard of them. Alaric's confusion increased. He'd been coming to this shop all his life, first in a pushchair, then as a toddler holding his mother's hand, for the past few years on his own or with his mates. The owners were the parents of one of his best friends. He'd often stayed to tea in the flat upstairs. Slept over a couple of times. He glanced about him, a reflexive check that he was where he'd intended to be, and noticed labels he'd missed or thought nothing of when passing them – Battle Creek Cornflakes, Heinz 59, Boulanger's Soups (like Campbell's in every detail but the name) – and that where a framed poster of the Queen usually hung there was one of an unfamiliar man in a grey suit.

'That'll be eight twenty-six,' the woman said.

He handed over the tenner Kate had given him. The note was half-way to the till when she looked at it, smiled frostily, and returned it.

'Good try.'

'What's wrong?'

The woman snorted. 'What's wrong!' She gripped the carrier – 'I'll put these back in a minute, shall I?' – and stashed it under the counter.

Red-faced, and very bewildered, he left the shop. The door buzzed contemptuously at his going.

Outside he moved along the pavement to be away from the woman's glare through the window. There was never much traffic in Eynesford and there was none now, not even any temporarily-parked cars or delivery vans, so he had a clear view of the street – a view he hadn't taken in when turning the corner from the lane. He reeled at what he saw. The buildings were taller than they ought to be, most of the doors were wider, and many of the windows were arched, like church windows. But it was the lines below the kerbs that clinched it. They were narrower than usual, and not double, but triple. And they were green, not yellow.

A curtain twitched in a window opposite. To avoid busybody eyes, he crossed the street to look in the bike shop while he tried to make sense of these anomalies. He stood before the big plate-glass window, not really focusing until it registered that the handlebars of every bike on show were equipped with small plasma screens. He'd also never seen a scooter like the one to the side of the main display. It had a very high seat, no wheels, and bore a sign which read: 'The digitalised Hoverscoot from The Independent Republic of Chechnya'.

He heard a car coming and turned from the window to watch its approach. It was an ordinary enough car, if not a model he could put a name to, but it wasn't the make or design that caused him to stare. It was the way it was being driven. On the wrong side of the road.

9: 39

Naia puzzled over the letter, particularly its statement that there'd been no Underwoods at Withern when Aldous U was her age. Having free access to the garden, and with such a first name, and that initial for his surname, he had to be an Underwood himself, so what was that all about?

With little expectation of it being relevant, she decided to try and discover the family name of the people who'd lived there from 1947 to 1963, the only period since its construction that Underwoods had not owned Withern Rise. She'd never enquired about them before in this or her original reality. For her, their occupation was best erased from Withern history, if only for what they did to the south garden. She'd seen the south garden as it was in the mid-1940s, albeit under water, and could tell even from that unflattering glimpse that it would have been a glorious place to walk and sit and think if those philistines hadn't stripped it of its trees and shrubs, dug over the flower beds and paths, laid grass for a tennis court. There was no tennis court today, or much indication that there'd ever been one, and with only the Family Tree standing to one side, the south garden was the least interesting part of the entire property. When that magnificent old oak was felled – as it looked like it would have to be – there'd be nothing there worth looking at, nothing at all.

Kate suggested that she visit Stone Town Hall, a good suggestion as it turned out, for there she learnt that copies of earlier deeds to many of the older houses, including Withern Rise, were archived and available for public scrutiny. A few minutes' search by a helpful clerk revealed that the family that had bought and lived at Withern Rise during the non-Underwood years was called Ravage. She almost laughed out loud at the aptness of that name, but its discovery was no more helpful than she'd expected in that it did not explain Aldous U's presence there in his youth. She reminded herself that she'd only seen the deeds for this reality and that her correspondent had spoken of her visiting him in another. But even that thought did not explain what a teenage boy called Aldous Underwood would be doing at a Withern Rise owned by a family other than his own – whatever the reality.

Alaric returned from the village rather more alert to his surroundings, but if there were any differences along the lane they were so few and slight that he couldn't be sure he wasn't inventing them. The side gate, now that he knew it was not the entrance to his garden, was another matter. His gate, in far better condition, was set into a six-foot-high brick wall that ran all the way down to the river. This one hung badly between the posts of a wooden fence so disregarded that, further along, two of the panels leant out dramatically from the top. He went to inspect these, then a little further to look at a panel that had broken free and fallen the other way, into the garden. This one had been there for some time. Weeds and grass had forced their way between the strips that formed it, and it was littered with twists of paper, bottles, and crushed drink cans presumably tossed in from the lane. Lengths of barbed wire had been strung inexpertly between the posts to which the panel had once been attached. A bit of old rag, ripped from the shirt of an intruder perhaps, hung from one of the barbs.

The grounds, as seen from here, were a mess. Where Kate did her best to keep everything in check, this Withern Rise's residents seemed to have given it up as a bad job a long time ago. Where plants had withered and fruit fallen, they'd been left to rot. Grass grew tall. Weeds flourished. There was a greenhouse, but most of the glass had been smashed. A generation must have passed since anything was cultivated in it. He could also see two very old cars, darkly rusted, one of them lacking a front wheel. Beyond these, on the grass where the south garden began, stood a small brown caravan that had seen better decades, and behind this a great many trees where at home there was only one.

He put his forehead against the wire to peer into the part of the garden that led to the gate he'd left by. All the way to the cemetery wall, where the vegetable garden should be, there was nothing but wild grass, swollen earth, and the twisted spectres of long-dead plants. How could he have failed to notice all that during his walk from the willow?

The willow. He recalled the dizzy spell when he went after the cat. That must have been when it happened. He considered the implications. Until now he'd thought that the only extant way into other realities was via the Family Tree, but suddenly the willow in the north garden was the way. It was years since he last sat or stood near the trunk of that willow, but there'd been no hint of anything like this then. Even Grandpa Rayner, though he'd described peculiar feelings he used to get in there as a boy, and hearing odd sounds, hadn't said anything about other realities. He might not have used such terminology, of course, but if he had found his way to an alternative Withern Rise wouldn't he have mentioned it? Well, maybe not, to a young boy.

Interested to see how this pitiful version of his home looked from the opposite end of the garden, Alaric walked back to the cemetery steps and followed the path through the graveyard to Withybank Lane, on the far side of which, as in his reality, there was a small housing estate, except that these houses were closer to mock-Jacobean than mock-Tudor. Turning right, reaching the head of the drive, he found that the five-bar gate had fallen or been bullied free of its hinges, to lie bound to the unweeded earth by ligatures of ivy. The drive's single track, which after a twist or two would open out in front of the house, was divided into three strips, the middle one, thick with matted grass untouched by wheels, standing up like a deformed spine. The trees, bushes and shrubs that lined the drive were impenetrable: no glimpses of the house from here! A fence similar to the one that defined the northern boundary stretched from the gate to the river, but this one had fared even more badly. The entire length of it, panel after panel, along with their supports, lay broken in the ribbon of wild wood formerly just inside it.

What Alaric did not know was that the one wall that bordered this version of the property already stood at the time of the house's construction. Until the 1880s the stretch of land between the river and the cemetery wall was wooded, primarily by willows. In the late 1920s the Eldon Underwoods of all other realities in which a Withern Rise had been built erected two additional boundary walls. The Eldon of this reality, and this only, choked to death on a chicken bone in 1924, whereupon his eldest surviving child, Larissa May, sold the property to Henry Rackenford, a local magistrate, who was pleased to leave it bounded by trees. The present fences were erected in 1958 by the Pilgrim-Hope family when they purchased Withern Rise from Rackenford's estate upon his death at the age of eighty-seven. The house was sold twice more after Dominic Pilgrim-Hope's assets were seized following his trial for embezzlement, first to a family of nine called O'Farrell, and finally, in 1989, to Stacey and Stephen Curtis. These days, her three grown-up children and her husband having long since flown the coop, only Mrs Curtis lived here. After almost fifty years the boundary fences would have been in a less than first-rate condition even if cared for, but as they had been

ignored by the owner for the last nine of those years –
during which they'd been ritually abused by local
vandals, drunks and malcontents – it wasn't altogether
surprising that they were now sinking into the earth.

Knowing nothing of this history, it depressed Alaric
that any Withern Rise could have been so reduced. He
went back through the cemetery to the side gate.
Concluding that the way to his reality was via the
willow, he lifted the rusty latch and looked for the
concealed path that ran along the north wall at
home, but saw only tangled scrub. The path to the
willow being so exposed, he cut across the overgrown
garden, running low as if dodging searchlights. He was
about half-way to the willow when an enormous
black Alsatian appeared at the corner of the house,
the River Room corner, and bounded towards him,
barking furiously. Alaric stopped in his tracks. Only
when a woman followed the dog, waving a stick and
screaming 'I've warned you young sods, I said I'd
set him on you next time, you asked for it!' did he
set off again, running with greater urgency than
he'd ever run in his life.

Plunging into the willow, he raced to the trunk,
struck it with his palms, and reached for something to
haul himself up by. His feet were barely off the ground
when the Alsatian's teeth closed on one of his trainers.

He kicked in terror, but the brute held on, snarling and tugging, dedicated to getting him down and setting about him properly. He swung the heel of his other foot, kicked again and again and again. The dog's jaws parted in pain and fury just as the branch snapped. Alaric hit the ground hard, but he was up in a trice, ready to run, run anywhere, when flight suddenly became unnecessary.

The dog was no more. And Mrs Curtis's cries of vengeance had ceased.

11: 43

Battered and cumbersome as it was, Aldous U was very attached to his typewriter. It would have been sensible to buy a more modern product – a wind-up Linux-K from Reality 467 or 470, for instance, or a solar-powered laptop from any one of half-a-dozen realities around the mid-two hundreds – but he enjoyed the physical effort of hammering those bolshie old keys, even if the result was not very refined. He'd acquired it years ago in a junk shop in the Eynesford of R229 (as he listed it at the time), staggered down the lane with it to that reality's Withern Rise, and slipped in the side gate, cautiously because he wasn't known there. From the gate, a lumbering rush to the crossing point, tiresomely situated in a bed of nettles behind the old tool-shed that had since been taken down in most realities; then the journey through the forest, where every obstruction brought an oath for his foolishness in buying the thing simply because the manufacturer's name tickled him. But later, when he'd cooled off and stretched his back, he was pleased that he'd made the effort.

He sat back from the typewriter. Fond of it as he was, he doubted he would take it with him. Too many other things to get out, and no helpers. He wished he knew precisely how long he had here. Going by the sky and the speed with which the vegetation was turning, not long at all. Over the next five or six days he would remove everything he really needed to the rooms he'd taken at the *Sorry Fiddler* in R36. Temporary rooms. Soon, months at most, he would have his house. Mustn't let it slip through his fingers, but he didn't want to seem predatory. Put in an offer in a day or two.

Something soft wound itself languorously around his legs. He bent to tickle the warm tortoiseshell fur. 'Where've you been this time, old lad?' There was more to the question than the words implied, for he had discovered a long time ago that cats, and this cat in particular, could pass through crossing points and return without any kind of device – something he himself could not do. What it was in a cat's physiology that allowed it to do this had at first intrigued him, but finding no explanation for the ability he had eventually settled for its being a fact of feline life. If he'd learnt nothing else over the years it was that some things would always be beyond his understanding, and contented himself with the knowledge that this cat cared enough for him to return to him time after time from his wanderings. No human had ever gone to such lengths to keep his company.

He was still stroking the creature's neck when he caught a movement outside. He straightened up and looked out, saw no one in the yard or at the edge of the forest, but imagined that one of the boys had been there. He recalled the day he saw the first of them, the stocky ginger-haired one. He'd been doing some weeding when something made him look up, and there he was. So surprised was he to see a human face where there'd never been one before that he cried out, which must have startled the lad, for he dived straight back into the undergrowth as though he'd been shot at. There'd been the odd sighting of him since, usually with one or more of the others who'd joined him later, but they'd all kept their distance and not responded when he called a greeting.

He'd felt sorry for the boys in the beginning. They were probably frightened, having no idea how they'd got here or how to get back to wherever they came from, their only shelter and source of food the forest itself. For a time he'd left provisions for them, brought in specially from one reality or another, along with matches, cooking implements, crockery and cutlery, but returning from an extended trip away* he found that they'd stolen from him, damaged his wall, trampled his garden. He did not renew the meal ticket. Whenever he caught sight of them now they glared belligerently as if he were their worst enemy. Young idiots. He was the only useful contact they were likely to find in this entire reality and they'd chosen to alienate him. With some success.

12: 47

Not at all confident as to what he would find outside of it, Alaric stepped clear of the willow. What he saw was as like his garden as any could be – as was the house like his house when he looked round the hawthorn hedge. Nevertheless, he proceeded nervously to the corner the Alsatian had leapt from, needing some verification that he was really home

---

* He'd been injured in R503, that most unstable of realities, and had to lay up for a while.

before meeting anyone. He rounded the corner and pulled up sharp. Kate. Down by the porch, kneeling on some sort of pad, fiddling with the white roses that grew there. Was it the Kate he knew, or some other? Should he back away, or—

Too late. She'd sensed him.

'Hello. Get everything?'

'I haven't been yet.'

'Well, no rush.'

She returned to her task. He watched her for half a minute before summoning his nerve and moving forward.

'Kate?'

It was the first time, in all these months, that he'd uttered her name in her presence. To him it felt almost impertinent. Not to her, though. She sat back, smiling.

'Alaric.'

'I'm—' He faltered.

'Yes?'

'I'm glad you're here.' Delivered in such a rush, it clearly startled her. 'With us,' he added, reddening, already retreating.

Kate remained quite still for some time after he'd gone. It was all she could do not to bawl her eyes out.

The fire, made up of dry twigs, grass and heaped leaves, pumped sparks into the night. Wood splintered and crackled. Originally, their fires had been started by striking a stone against the blade of Scarry's pen-knife, a tedious, hit-and-miss process; then, for a while, there'd been the matches, but when they ran out and were not replaced they were forced to return to their former system – until Gus O'Brien arrived with his cigarette lighter. It was the lighter rather than Gus's personality that brought him a welcome. He was Ric's age, but seemed older, being much more self-assured, lacking any degree of self-doubt. He was extremely thin, with long arms that swung as he loped along, and skeletal fingers that moved ponderously, like the limbs of a sleepy spider. His eyes were small and dark, quite piercing if they picked you out, and his hair so fair that in certain lights it seemed almost white. He parted his hair in the middle, and when he bent forward it fell on either side of his face, shadowing his sharp features. Ric had disliked Gus at first sight, and not warmed to him since.

They were preparing their evening meal on the pitted apron of rock in front of Scarry's house when the pipes started. They'd heard them before, irregularly, always in the evening or at night, so the sound did not startle them; but, as always, chatter ended and heads tilted as the breathy sound floated zephyr-light through the trees. Only Gus and Scarry responded negatively, Gus with a growled 'Jesus Christ!' and a covering of the head, Scarry with a sneer and a contemptuous gob into the fire. Ric did not share their disdain for these musical interludes. The playing wasn't particularly accomplished, but the panpipes' wistful character soothed his mind. He guessed from the softening of the younger boys' features that they were similarly charmed, though neither the music nor its effect was ever discussed.

There was also a response from some of the forest's other life. On those nights that the man from the stone house set a chair outside his door and breathed into the pipes, birds that kept quiet and still during the day would stir. Out of the dusk or darkness they would warble and chuckle and caw and screech in a rising cacophony that would amuse Ric, bring a groan from Scarry, and turn Gus apoplectic. Tonight, as the pipes played on and the cries and squawks reached a crescendo, Gus jumped up, shouted 'This is driving me nuts!', and plunged into the bushes. Scarry, attempting similar rage – a pale imitation – took his own leave shortly afterwards, in a different direction.

The mood among the remaining four was lighter for Gus and Scarry's absence, but they went about their business as though deaf to the sounds that had driven them away. When the playing ceased and the birds calmed down, the silence that replaced the clamour was stark by comparison. Needing to take the edge off it – and purge the musings the pipes had stimulated – Ric jumped up and strode to where the three boys sat minding the white squirrel sizzling on a spit. Although larger than any squirrel they'd encountered before, there still wasn't enough flesh on it to satisfy six stomachs, so care must be taken with every edible scrap and morsel.

'Watch it doesn't burn,' Ric said. 'There's nothing else.'

'Sure there is,' a thin, amused voice said.

Something thudded at his feet. He jumped back.

'What's this?'

Gus jerked into the firelight. 'What does it look like?'

Ric peered – and recoiled. 'It's a cat!'

'It's meat.'

He inspected the dead animal. 'It...it's not...?'

'Yep. This'll keep him quiet for a while.'

'Oh, you reckon, do you?'

Gus squinted at him. 'Something bothering you?'

Ric withdrew, unnerved by the sardonic grin in the shuddering firelight. They were the same height, and he was broader, but he had no doubt that Gus, with his thinly-veiled eagerness for conflict, could take him, and revel in the taking.

'Whassat?' Scarry, returning from the trees, adjusting his belt.

'Fresh rations,' Gus said.

Scarry bent over the cat. Recognising the fur, he laughed, but with some unease. To cover this, he picked the cat up by the tail and dangled it over the fire. Fur sizzled, and caught. He continued to hold it while small flames crept up the body from the head, stripping it hair by hair. When the only uncharred fur was at the end of the tail, he laid the carcass beside the fire, almost tenderly now it was on the menu.

'How's the squirrel doing?' Gus asked.

'Looks done,' said Jonno.

'Get it off then and do this.'

The boys weren't keen to touch the cat, so Scarry picked it up again, swung it before their eyes. Hag looked like he was fighting tears. The other two tried to look amused, but their eyes betrayed them. They prised the squirrel off the spit, fingers dancing on the hot flesh, while Scarry drove the skewer down the cat's throat, the length of its body, forcing it out the end with leering effort. He tossed the result into Badger's lap. Badger shrieked and jumped up. The skewered cat rolled onto the rocky ground. Scarry told the boys to stop feckin' about and get on with it.

'What do you think he'll do when he finds out?' Ric wondered aloud.

'He won't find out if it's eaten,' Scarry said.

'He will if we hang the leftovers outside his door,' said Gus.

Scarry chuckled, again uneasily. 'Yeah.'

'He might come after us,' a small frightened voice said: little Hag.

'Hope he does,' Gus said.

Ric glanced at the boys. Noted their alarm. They didn't know – none of them knew – what Gus O'Brien was capable of.

FLASH 2

The strain of driving through the rain and the dark, the constant glare of oncoming headlights, was getting to her. Pulling in at a service station for a break, she found all the spaces around the restaurant taken. She parked as near as she could, clambered out with the usual difficulty, and made an ungainly dash through more puddles than she missed.

She wasn't really hungry, but she hadn't eaten for hours, so after seating herself at one of the faux-marble tables by the window and logging her ID with the tabscan, she tapped an extra key on the selection pad. Thirty seconds later a Fairtrade mocha and a cinnamon Danish rose up on the tablewaiter. In spite of the speed of delivery the pastry turned out to be as stale as the drink was stewed. 'Fucking dump,' she thought, only realising that she'd said it out loud when a bald man at a nearby table grinned agreement. She toyed with the Danish, sipped the foul beverage, and gazed bleakly through her fragmented image in the streaming black window.

It bothered her, what she was about to do. By insisting on the location of her child's birth, and where it was to grow up, she was forcing events, foisting a whole rack of unforeseeable consequences on it and, by extension, on a great many others as yet unborn. Since her teens she'd been acutely aware of how a life can jump tracks with a word, an involuntary movement, any one of a thousand tiny decisions made or not made on a given or ungiven day. At sixteen her life had changed radically, tragically, and her school work, along with her confidence, had suffered terribly. She'd rallied because she'd had to, but even with the second, ultimately more pleasing, upheaval later that year her work had never recovered sufficiently for her to achieve the grades she would have obtained in her original reality. Career choices thus reduced, a series of nothing-much jobs followed until a vague interest in archaeology coupled with a natural facility with pen and pencil brought a small commission to illustrate some found objects. This led to other commissions, and eventually to a three-month contract at the Vindolanda site on Hadrian's Wall where she'd met Donald Lomas, a twenty-seven-year-old volunteer helping with the excavations. She and Don had lived together for just over four years, towards the end of which she discovered that he'd been screwing around for at least two of them. She had moved out of their flat and his life ten days before learning of her condition, which, wanting nothing more to do with him, she'd decided to keep to herself. The child would be hers alone, and would bear the Underwood name.

And here was the point, or part of it. If not for the succession of abstract occurrences that had conveyed her to the wandering eye of Don Lomas, she would have gone in another direction entirely, to a different relationship, more than one perhaps, and not, this unpleasant October night, be heading for Withern Rise to give birth to his child.

She shoved the coffee and the plate away and got up.

'Back into the night, eh?' the man at the nearby table said.

'Yeah. Fun.'

But first, to the pretentiously-labelled 'Femmes'. Checking herself in the mirror after leaving the cubicle, she could not ignore the shadows under her eyes and the lines at the corners which had little to do with laughter. The unsubtle wall lighting also picked out silver threads in her damp hair. Until February she'd *always worn her hair long, but because Don had liked it that way the week after she walked out on him she'd had the bulk of it lopped off. In the mirror, with these harsh shadows, these lines, she looked like an over-the-hill pixie.*

She was on her way back to the car, rushing head down into the rain, when it came to her that by checking her appearance in the mirror she'd left the restaurant a minute or two later than she would have if she had not. She was about to rejoin the motorway x-number of vehicles on from that point. One of the cars or lorries in the new stream of traffic might be driven by someone who'd drunk more than he should, or one of his tyres might blow, making him lose control and cause an accident in which she would be a fatality. She and her unborn child. On the other hand, something of the sort might have happened if she'd left sooner rather than later. The face-check of the haggard pixie might just have saved their two lives. There was no telling which departure would have been to their best advantage. There never was.

Part Two
THE WILD

1: 36

'Bit early to look over a house, isn't it?' Ivan huffed.

'The agent said it's their only chance this week. From here they're off to some relatives for a few days.'

'So why don't they wait till they get back?'

'Maybe they don't want to risk losing it, I didn't ask. Where are you going?'

'The shop, where else?'

'But it's not even nine.'

'You don't think I'm staying here while strangers traipse round my home, do you?'

'You obviously expect me to.'

'You're better at things like that.'

'I've never shown anyone round a house before.'

'You'll pick it up.'

He closed the door behind him.

They arrived at ten past: an amiable middle-aged couple with a babe-in-arms and a daughter in her early teens. Alex longed to ask them to remove their shoes before going upstairs, particularly to the bedrooms, but didn't know how to without seeming rude. The parents seemed to like the house from the first, but when the woman murmured as they went along the hall, 'Big, isn't it?' little more needed to be said. They did the full tour, however, inspecting every room, every built-in cupboard, the woman commenting favourably on the furnishings, various ornaments, the views of the garden, while the man seemed content to smile and add the occasional word of agreement. The daughter, saying even less, looked bored, while the baby whimpered all the way round, and smelt foul.

After they'd driven away, promising to think about it, Alex phoned Ivan. He said he'd ring her back, which meant that he had customers. He returned the call about fifteen minutes later.

'You rang to tell me they weren't interested?' he said, when she gave this opinion.

'I can't be certain, but I'll be surprised if we hear from them again.'

'Well, there'll be others.'

'Hope so.'

He detected something in her voice. 'What is it, Lexie?'

'Nothing. Just…you know.'

He wasn't sure that he did, but he made the appropriate noises in soft tones, and clicked off with a relief he did not like to admit to.

2: 47

'Why are you still here?' Alaric asked, finding his father in the kitchen when he went down for breakfast.

'Overslept.' Ivan finger-and-thumbed two crisp slices of wholemeal from the toaster. 'Sat up too late last night watching that stupid bloody film.'

Alaric poured cereal and milk into a bowl. They'd both just sat down to eat when Kate looked in the window.

'Come and see this.'

'Why didn't you wake me?' Ivan demanded.

'Wake you? Since when was waking you in the job description?'

'Kate, you know I have a shop to run.'

'Didn't think of it. Busy.'

'Doing what?'

'The garden. Come and look.'

'I can look at the garden any time.'

'I don't mean the garden. There's an injured toad here.'

'Well, if it croaks it won't be the first time.'

'Come on. Both of you.'

With a sigh apiece, they got up and went outside, flinching at the brightness of the day. They joined Kate at the edge of the drive, on her haunches beside a pile of bricks Ivan had had delivered for a bit of wall he planned to build sometime-never. They bent to inspect the toad. It was large and green, gulping hard, staring helplessly up at them.

'Looks like it's been mauled,' Kate said. Alaric told her of the cat he'd seen in the garden yesterday. 'That's probably it then. Cats!'

'Why is this of interest?' Ivan asked.

'Why? The poor thing's suffering.'

'It's not a pet. These things happen in the wild.'

'The wild? Your garden?'

'We can't be responsible for every creature that hangs around it. Not exactly invited guests, are they?'

Kate leant over the toad, trying to soothe it but not liking to touch it. Alaric watched her. She was so concerned. No idea what to do, but concerned.

Just like Mum would have been.

'I wonder if we could get it to a vet,' Kate murmured.

'Vet?' Ivan said. 'How much do you think one of *those* would cost?'

'Well, we can't just leave it to *suffer*, Ivan.'

'No. You're right. Move aside.'

She obeyed, shuffling to one side without rising.

'What are you thinking?' she asked.

A brick came down hard. A small squelch.

Ivan stood up. 'Problem solved,' he said. 'Now. Mind if I finish my toast?'

He stalked back to the house. As he reached the step he stopped suddenly and gripped his left arm, but within thirty seconds he was back at the table, munching toast, sipping tea.

Kate and Alaric had not moved. Their eyes hadn't left the brick. You wouldn't have known there was anything under it.

3: 39

There was a chill to the mornings now, but still Aldous woke raring to experience every moment of every day, whatever the temperature or weather. The injustice of his life's brevity did not weigh heavily, though the loss of his immediate family saddened him. Naia had told him as much as she'd been able to find out about them: that the house, along with his father's boat-yard, had been sold after the war and that Withern Rise (but not the boat-yard) had been bought back years later by his brother Rayner; that his eldest sister Ursula had married at some point, produced two daughters (whose current whereabouts were unknown) and moved to Canada. All she could tell him about his youngest sister, Mimi, was what Alex had discovered when compiling the Underwood family tree: that she might or might not have married but had had a child at some point. Aldous often thought about impish, high-spirited little Mimi. She was nine the last time he saw her. Seemed no time ago at all to him, but she'd be in her late sixties now. All those missing years. If she was still alive, what sort of life had she had? Where was she today? What was her situation? And why hadn't she been there when he woke from his long sleep? Why hadn't *anyone* been there?

Kate had got on to the nursing home where he'd spent most of his life, and nagged them until they provided, grudgingly, all the information they had in their database on the family. It wasn't much. His mother had visited regularly through all the years of

Aldous's confinement until she died in her seventies. The trust fund she had set up to take care of him had been on the point of running out when he woke. His restoration to full wakefulness had come just in time. As Aldous had very little money of his own, Kate took it upon herself to make sure that he received the state pension that a person of his apparent maturity was entitled to. His unusual progression towards his present age, without a single insurance contribution along the way, had proved a stumbling block, but she'd persevered to such rewarding effect that Naia was rather proud of her.

Aldous didn't say as much – though he couldn't help hinting at it – but he hated what had become of the area since he was officially a child here. It was all so ugly now, so vulgar, with such a cramped air, strutted by bullet-eyed youths and large, loud girls, the pavements spattered with grey blobs of chewing gum and spittle, vomit occasionally, and wherever there was grass there was litter. Withern Rise, too, looked slightly jaded to his eyes, and the garden far less abundant and bountiful than it had been in the 1940s. Mr Knight did his best with the garden, but he was only part-time and not as knowledgeable or as painstaking as his father must have been. And it wasn't really a working garden these days. All that was required of it was that it did not offend the eye too much. The panorama from the front porch, for instance, was largely unobstructed by the bushes and hedges and informal structures that had once added such character. In the old days the drifting eye was pleasantly hindered at every turn. There were more trees then, plants of all kinds and description, much more colour, and more birds (and hence more birdsong), there being more for them to perch on, nest among, lay their eggs in.

The Withern Rise Aldous had known in the 1930s and '40s had been a complete world to him and his sisters and brother. There was the village and the town, but very little beyond as far as they were aware or cared. Even the war hadn't really encroached. News bulletins about the conflict came out of a box which was switched off when the listeners had heard enough. Almost everything that mattered was just a few steps away, easily within reach – or it came to them. The village barber and a hairdresser from Stone would visit regularly to attend to everyone's hair. There were deliveries by the baker, the grocer, the butcher, the fishmonger, but most other fare came from the garden itself. Mr Knight grew their potatoes, carrots, cabbages, marrows, parsnips, lettuces, cucumbers, tomatoes and radishes (Aldous had never liked radishes); and there were apples and pears, strawberries, raspberries, gooseberries and redcurrants, while a plum tree wound itself around the garage walls. In addition, they had trees that bore walnuts, hazelnuts, sweet chestnuts, and the crunchy little cobnuts that he loved most of all. And there were eggs, of course, from the chicken run. Father and Grandpa used to hunt rabbits on the Coneygeare too (much wilder then, more expansive, not bordered by houses and flats with a pub on the corner). Aldous would go with them sometimes, excited by the bark of the shotguns; such big guns for such small quarry. And then there was that beautiful white goat of theirs. Flo, they called her, because she produced such quantities of milk. He remembered the day – he was seven – when he finally got the joke. This was long after Flo had been dispatched. It came to him one teatime, and he spluttered his milk all over the table and was sent to bed straightaway with a smack.

His childhood at Withern Rise so filled Aldous's mind these days that he was sometimes hard pressed to separate past from present. He would be strolling around the garden, stop suddenly and close his eyes, smell flowers that were no longer there, hear the squeals of Mimi and Ray scampering nearby, or their laughter as they pushed one another on the swing that hung from the old apple tree. Then – as this morning –

the creak of the wheelbarrow, iron wheels on gravel. Opening his eyes, he expected, for a happy second, to find everything as it used to be, as it should be, with him allowed to act like a kid again, run about, climb trees, be as silly and loud as he liked, Maman at an upstairs window, Father chatting to Mr Knight, the future still waiting its turn.

But no. It was gone. All of it.

The wheelbarrow that crunched by on the path, though the same wheelbarrow, was pushed by today's Mr Knight who, uncharacteristically, merely grunted in passing. No Mimi and Ray, no swing, no apple tree, no more childhood.

Aldous blinked several times, then dragged disconsolate feet away, as if from the past, across the bland south garden to the strip of wilderness that ran from the river to the main gate – all that remained of the array of trees and bushes that had once covered this portion of the grounds. Virtually untouched since the Underwood name was returned to the deeds in the early 1960s, this ribbon of chaos was rarely entered, though it would never have occurred to anyone to tidy or clear it, it being all there was, now, of the old south garden. Aldous had loved the south garden as it was back then. So had the others. Riding their trikes and scooters through it, hiding in it, having little picnics together in secret bowers, small worlds away from grown-up regimes and bedtime.

When he heard Naia's voice raised in a shout, he turned to see her breaking out of the bushes that lined the drive. Mr Knight, way down in the vegetable garden now, must also have heard her, for he looked up from his work, which currently seemed to be pummelling the earth with the heaviest spade he could find.

'What's up?' Aldous called.

'There was a man in the drive!'

They started towards one another.

'What did he want?'

'He didn't stop to say. I only wanted to speak to him.' They met in the middle of the lawn. 'I've seen him before,' Naia said. 'Watching the house, taking pictures. And looking through these.'

There was an old pair of binoculars in her hand. Brass binoculars.

'You took them off him?'

'No, he dropped them as he skedaddled.'

'I had a pair like that,' Aldous said.

'Did you? Well, I suppose they were quite common a few years back. Now I think of it, I've seen some myself, somewhere…'

It came to her even as she said it. It was back in

February, her first time in this reality, when it was still Alaric's. There'd been no one at home and she'd taken the opportunity to look around, found them in the double wardrobe in the master bedroom. She hadn't seen them since, or given them a thought.

'May I see?' She handed them over. 'Look.' He indicated the letters 'LU' engraved between the eye-pieces.

'Maker's initials?' Naia said.

'My Aunt Larissa's.'

'Your aunt's?'

'These are the glasses she gave me on my eleventh birthday.'

Naia stared, at the binoculars, at him, back at the binoculars. Then she whirled about and raced to the Family Tree. She felt in the message hole and found an envelope which, as before, had her name on it. She did not go back to Aldous, but round the side of the house, to the landing stage, where she sat to read the directions to the reality of Aldous U.

4: 43

Early that morning, before anyone else was up, Gus had gone to the house in the clearing and hung the cat's remains on the door. He'd left the stripped legs on, and the tail, the charred head with its blank button eyes, and waited in the bushes for the man to come out. 'He burst into tears!' he crowed, telling of this. 'God, it was a scream.'

'Sounds it,' Ric muttered.

The ridiculously wide grin switched off. 'What's that?'

'Nothing.'

'Something to say, say it, jerk-off.'

'I've got nothing to say.'

'I have,' Scarry said.

Gus switched the grin back on. 'What's that, Cap?'

Almost from the first he'd called Scarry 'Cap', sometimes 'Captain', his way of acknowledging his status.

Scarry said: 'I think you're getting above yourself.'

'Above myself, Cap?'

'Didn't check with me first.'

'About the cat, you mean? Hanging it up?'

'Yeah. Hanging it up.'

'I thought you liked the idea.'

'Not the point. You check with me 'fore you do stuff. Right?'

Gus stared at him expressionlessly for a moment, and, slowly then, said: 'Right. Yeah. Sorry if I was out of line, Cap.'

"Kay. Long as that's straight.'

As Scarry turned away, Gus's eyes, dark and cold, flicked around the group. They'd seen him put in his place and he didn't like it. Even Ric found it hard not to shiver.

5: 39/43

Following the first of the typed instructions, Naia went to the willow in the north garden. There she found, looped into the ivy that twirled the old trunk, the small pouch she'd been told to look for. She was convinced that the man who'd run from her in the drive was Aldous U. Too much of a coincidence that she'd seen him three times now – the first two times in June – so close to the Family Tree, where the envelopes were deposited.

The pouch was nothing special, a piece of ordinary green cloth closed with black cord. The number forty-three was embroidered into the material. Without bothering to speculate on the significance of the number, or to inspect its contents, she shoved the pouch in a pocket of her jeans and went round the trunk to follow the next instruction, which she'd already made up her mind not to follow unconditionally. The note – just a few lines this time – had told her to take a single step forward from there at two pm, not just after eleven in the morning. There were two reasons why she chose not to wait. The first was that she was impatient to see what would happen; the second, that she didn't like being given orders by someone who lacked the grace to speak to her face to face.

She experienced a fleeting rush of disorientation when she took the step. Believing herself prepared for anything, what she did not expect when her foot came down was to find herself in a gloomy, eerily quiet forest whose odour reminded her of the mulch pit in a generally-avoided corner of the garden.

She'd barely got over the shock when she began wondering what to do next. Deciding that she couldn't hang around here till two when Aldous U had said he'd be here to introduce himself, it occurred to her that she knew nothing about him other than what she'd seen as he scuttled away from her: a tall, jumpy, red-haired man unlike any Underwood she knew of. How did she know he hadn't lured her here for purposes he'd been fantasising about since he first started watching her, whenever that was? She considered stepping back across the point at which she'd come into this place, but hesitated. There'd been nothing in any of his missives to suggest that he was a stalker with dark intentions; and besides, this was such a different reality: could she turn her back on it without even taking a look around?

Knowing the answer to this even as she posed the question, she uttered a tentative 'Hello...?' The lack of any kind of response in such profound silence was unsettling. Determined not to be cowed by nothing at all, she looked about her more critically. Winter was still some way off, but all the trees and bushes, every clump and cluster of leaves, appeared far less healthy than they should. So dull, so downcast, so...weary.

She shook herself. Get going. Explore. But which way? There being no signposts she could take her pick and be wrong whichever way she went; but she chose a direction and set off. With the bushes between the trees so unruly, the trees themselves so tightly-packed, she had to push and sidle and bully her way along. Hoping constantly to see a break ahead, she was frustrated when each shove and plunge revealed only more of the same. And so her progress continued for some time until, without warning, she burst out of the forest and crashed into a waist-high drystone wall. Pausing – because she had to – she saw that beyond the wall was a sizeable clearing, in the approximate centre of which stood the strangest, most improbable house she'd ever seen.

The walls of the house were composed of lumps of blue-grey rock, some no bigger than a rugby ball, many the size of a large sack of coal, all jammed together with little if any attempt at uniformity. The roof was a sagging tent of irregular slates tufted with yellow moss, the chimney a careless accretion of stones that ran a perpendicular course from the ground to the roof at one end of the building. Red ivy clambered and delved wherever it pleased across these grossly uneven surfaces, and here and there small weeds sprouted. An old rain barrel, bound by rusty iron bands, stood in a yard bulging with wayward grasses and frail-looking flowers. Half-a-dozen pots contained rather healthier plants, however, one of which, a magnificent turquoise bloom, was so luminous as to seem quite out of place.

Some way along, to her right, there was a wooden gate in the wall. Having no doubt that she'd found the home of Aldous U, Naia went to this and lifted the latch. A couple of hens, pecking half-heartedly, scattered as she shoved the gate back. She closed it quietly behind her, not liking to disturb the stillness that carried over from the forest, and started along a dirt path towards a faded blue door overhung with a listless, grey-petalled rambling rose. Old tales filled her mind as she walked, of wolves in granny caps and shawls awaiting visitors, the porridge and chairs and beds of bears, witches luring children into hovels and ovens. *Steady, Nai,* she said to herself, *you're losing it.*

Drawing near, she saw a large padlock on the door; the kind you see on a garden shed. She wondered why a padlock. Didn't they have standard door locks here? But a padlock meant that there was no one at home, so there was no point in knocking. She went to the window to the right of the door, which she discovered was made not of glass but of thick transparent acrylic. She thought it must be the quality or the age of this material that gave it its yellow cast, but on turning to assess the world it attempted to reflect she realised what she had not realised between the forest and the house: that the sky itself, and hence the light that issued from it, was of a similar hue.

Making a cave of her hands, she peered through the window. Too dark to see much in there. Stepping away, her eyes drifted to a small wooden plaque on the other side of the door, half-concealed by the trailing end of the rambling rose. She went to the plaque, uncovered it, and saw the words carved into it. This eccentric, thrown-together excuse for a house was called Withern Rise.

Alaric's curiosity about the willow in the north garden was tempered with anxiety. Unless yesterday was a fluke, the tree could be the route to more than one reality. On the other hand it might lead only to the reality with the Alsatian. The mauled toad might have got off lightly compared to him if those eager jaws were given a second snap at him.

Undecided whether to take a chance or take no chance at all, he had once again gone to the landing stage. He often ended up there when bothered by something or needing to think, even though it was at the only side of the property that was completely open to public scrutiny. A line of ducks scattered as a small cruiser chugged by, a shirtsleeved man in a cap at the wheel, partner and young daughter lounging in the stern. The woman smiled at Alaric. The child waved. He raised his hand, but too late, the boat had moved on, the tidal ribbons of its wake running for the reeds that crowded the banks.

What to do? Chance it or not?

After peering into every window of the house and still making out very little inside, Naia completed her circuit and returned to the gate. Two o'clock was still over two hours away. She couldn't just stand here till then, waiting for Aldous U to turn up. She entered the forest at the point at which she'd emerged, and set off, attempting to retrace her steps, straining to pick out indications that she'd passed that way. Such was her concentration that she was unaware of the slight movement of leaves about her as she went, and unprepared for the eventual ''Ello, darling' that preceded a rush and flurry and a pair of wiry arms locking about her, hauling her off her feet. Only when she lay upon rough ground between trampled bushes did fear kick in. Figures blurred about her in the drear light.

'Who is she?'

'What's she doin' here?'

'I thought we was the only ones.'

'Tasty, eh, Cap? Do with summa this, couldn't you?'

'Feckin' right I could.'

'Better tie her down.'

'Do what?'

'We don't want her running off, now do we?'

'No. Right. Ric, tie her hands.'

Behind her, an uncertain voice that she was too diverted to recognise: 'Hey, no, I don't know about this...'

'Yeah, well you wouldn't, would you? Just do it. Right, Cap?'

'Yeah. Do it.'

'There's nothing to tie her with.'

'So hold her, hold her!'

The one behind her sat her up and gripped her wrists with both hands, while the two who'd done most of the talking squatted in front of her. One was a heavy-set youth, eighteen, nineteen, not very bright-looking; the other, possibly younger but more confident, very rangy, grinned at her like he'd had his mouth surgically stretched. Three other boys, still children really, stood watching, glancing nervously at one another. The only one she'd not yet seen was the one who held her wrists behind her. In all this she'd made little sound, but she made up for it now, with an angry torrent of indignation as she lashed out with her feet, one of which struck a knee. The youth with the wide grin toppled backwards. The heavier one gave a half-laugh, shifted out of reach, and asked her where she'd come from.

'What's it to you?'

'Jus' showin' an interest.'

'Let me go!'

She squirmed furiously, but failed to pull her hands free. The one she'd kicked got up and stooped over her. Leaning, he looked even thinner. Narrow chest and shoulders in a torn black T-shirt, greasy fair hair flopping around his narrow bum-fluff jaw, hooding the small eyes that gazed at her with the amusement of one who knows he has the upper hand, and intends to use it.

'What do you want?' she demanded, as steadily as she could.

His laugh sent shivers through her. 'One guess.' She made to kick him again, but he grabbed her ankle, pushed it down hard. She squealed.

'Don't break it,' the heavier boy said. 'Better in one piece.'

The pressure eased. 'Are you on your own?'

She scowled. 'On my own, here? What do you take me for?'

'Who else then? Other girls?'

'Men. My brothers. All I have to do is shout.'

'How many?'

'Brothers? Four.'

'Four brothers, all here? What are their names?'

'Their names?'

'They do have names, don't they?'

'Of course they have names!'

'So…?'

Four names trotted off one after the other might have made a difference, but for once Naia's imagination deserted her. Of the hundreds of male names she'd heard in her life, of the dozens she was very familiar with, not one came to her in this moment of duress. Gus O'Brien's unnaturally wide grin returned.

'Just as I thought.'

He kicked her legs apart and dropped between them; reached for the buckle of her belt. Unable to pull away, Naia twisted onto one hip. He forced her back, pressed her down, grabbed the buckle.

'Hold her!'

Jonno and Hag rushed forward, one each side, threw their weight onto her legs. She cried out in pain. Gus tore her belt apart, released the button of her jeans, yanked them down past her crotch. She fought insanely. Hag and Jonno clung to her legs as if their lives depended on it.

'Captain!'

Scarry moved in, lugging Badger, who he flung to Jonno's aid while he gripped Naia's other leg alongside Hag. Gus unzipped his jeans, and after a slight tussle revealed an object of wonder to the young boys. Even

Scarry gulped. The sight had a different effect on Naia. Her arms flew free; her released fists flailed with some success; there were shouts of pain – all of which did nothing to daunt Gus. He tore her pants, scratched her belly with long, dirty fingernails, and, holding her down with one hand, pushed himself forward. He was almost there when, following a splintering thud and a yelp, he toppled sideways. Scarry and Hag scampered out of the way just in time to avoid being crushed. Badger and Jonno also jumped back. Shocked eyes turned to Ric, standing there with a broken branch in his hand.

'Holy shit,' Scarry whispered.

Naia was already on her feet, hauling her jeans up. When her torn pants caught in the zip, she left it, fastened the belt while looking about for the best way out of there before her assailant recovered. But Gus was already recovering. Tucking away his diminished article, he pulled himself upright, snarling at the one who'd deprived him of his pleasure – the one whose face Naia now saw for the first time.

'Alaric!'

This brought a gasp in return. Disadvantaged by surprise, Ric fell easily under Gus's attack, covering his groin and as much else as he could while the enraged youth delivered kick after kick to any part the toes and heels of his boots could reach. Believing that she knew the one who had come to her aid, Naia might have taken his side had not a strong hand gripped her arm from behind and tugged her away. She made to spin round and fight off this new enemy, but before she could complete the turn she was whisked from the scene and running through undergrowth, weaving between trees, propelled from behind. Every step and stumble of the way she demanded to know who it was that forced her onward, but received no word of reply as he swerved and twisted her along a path she could not identify but which he clearly knew very well.

In minutes, reaching a certain spot, she was brought to a halt, but before she could finally confront her silent guide, he gave her a small shove which forced her to make one more step: a step which despatched her to a willow in a north garden, where, before she could catch her breath, she collided with one of the very last people she might have expected to find there.

8: 47

Eventually, reasoning that fear of the possible with no real knowledge of the probable is a pretty lame approach to anything, Alaric went to the willow. The leaves swished back into place as he passed through them and walked determinedly to the trunk. Not daring to pause for fear of losing his nerve, he stepped boldly round it – and crashed into Naia as she hurtled from the forest reality. The shock was mutual, though typically, while trying to claw back recently-expelled breath, she overcame it first.

'How did you get here before me?'

'Before you?'

'And how come you look so…? Hang on.'

She explored his face, his clothes.

'What?' he said.

'You're not him.'

'Not who?'

She skipped this, too full of her own questions to accommodate his. 'You know about this tree? What it can do?'

'Well…got an idea.'

She moved away from the trunk, not wanting to be drawn back into the world she'd just fled; the hands of the unsavoury types who dwelt there.

'When did you get here?' she asked.

'Get here?'

'Get here, get here,' she said irritably. 'Am I talking in hieroglyphics or something?'

He neither rose to her scorn nor answered her. Two could play at this. 'What was the big rush all about?'

'I was running. No choice. God, I wish I knew what he was up to.'

'Who?'

'Aldous U. He leaves these notes for me.'

'Notes?'

She frowned at him. 'You don't have an Aldous U?'

'The only Aldous I know of is the one who built Withern.'

'And Grandpa Rayner's brother,' she reminded him.

'I didn't know Grandpa had a brother.'

For a moment she thought he was having her on, but then recalled another time she'd made that assumption.

'When did we last meet?'

'You know bloody well when. February.'

'Not June?'

'June?'

'The Floods?' she prompted. '1945?'

'What the hell are you on about?'

'You were flooded, weren't you?'

'Yes, but…1945?'

She said: 'Let's get into the light.'

'Is that a good idea?'

'We'll stick to this end. But if we're seen,' she added, swimming through the leaves, 'we'd better part company without a fond farewell.'

Thanks to the tall hedge this side of the garage, their corner of the garden was not visible from the house, so they could not be seen from it. Naia dropped to the grass and crossed her legs at the ankle, outer thighs and calves flat on the ground, forgetting that she hadn't fixed her zip. When Alaric also sat, facing her, the combination of flaring zip and vaguely masculine posture disturbed him in ways he could not have articulated.

'What was that about June?'

'Are you sure we didn't meet then?' she said.

'I think I'd have remembered.'

'Well if it wasn't you it was another Alaric. One who had the same memories of February.'

He already knew of one other Alaric, though he hadn't passed this on. He didn't pass it on now. 'Was that who you thought I was just now?'

'I thought you were him *and* the one back there.'

'Back there?'

'I'm guessing,' she said slowly, 'that the June Alaric and that one aren't the same.' She leant back on her hands. Her fly gaped. 'The one I just met looked like he'd given up haircuts and washing and changing his clothes, and I think he was thinner. If I'm right, if he isn't the June Alaric, it means there are three of you.'

Four, he thought, purposefully locking eyes with her to thwart gravity.

'This last one,' he said. 'Did you meet him in your reality or his?'

'Not mine,' she answered. 'We were in a wood. A forest. What a place. So unhealthy-looking. Smelt horrible. I don't envy him if he lives there. And those friends of his! I was lucky to get out of there with my—'

'Oh, *there* you are!'

They turned their heads: Kate, coming round the hedge.

Naia jumped up. 'Time for that swift departure, methinks.'

He also got up, less hurriedly.

'Your dad just phoned,' Kate said. 'I have to go to Higham Grey to look at some possible stock for him.'

'Go on then,' Alaric whispered – to Naia.

'Go on yourself. Quick, or she'll see us close up.'

He stepped forward, putting himself in front of her.

'What are you doing?' she hissed.

'Keep back,' he said. 'And keep quiet.'

Kate reached them, tried to look round him. 'Who's this?'

'Just a girl from school.'

Naia stumbled in shock, literally stumbled, creating

a new distance which afforded Kate a good look at the state of her zip. Embarrassed, she rushed the essentials of her mission: 'Your dad told me to ask you to be here between one and two, he's expecting a package from a dealer, couriered, which'll have to be signed for. He can't get away, so could you do that?'

'I might not be here between one and two.'

'Oh. Well. Up to you. I passed it on.'

She forced a smile and walked briskly away.

Naia was staring wildly about her when Alaric turned to her. 'It isn't mine?' she said, and confirmed it at once. 'It isn't mine!'

Then she was running again, running back to the willow, diving through the leaves. Only when she was inside did he think to go after her, but on also plunging through he found himself alone there.

Subdued as the light was, he noticed a small pouch on the ground. He picked it up. She must have dropped it in her haste. Haste. If he was quick he might follow her. Could it work that way? He hoped so. So much to catch up on, talk about, understand. He went round the trunk. There was some disorientation as his foot came down, and then he stood on ground easily distinguishable from his own.

He was in a densely-wooded forest. Which smelt bad.

Another family to view the house already. She'd never have any time to herself at this rate. These were a Mr and Mrs Peterson and Mr Peterson's widowed mother, who it appeared was going to be living with them. They too remarked upon the size of the place, but with rather less awe, informing Alex that they had a fifteen-year-old son and a daughter in her twenties who still lived with them, and that they liked to have friends and relatives to stay, which made Withern Rise 'perfect'. Mrs Peterson senior, a bustling sparrow of a woman in her seventies, was obsessed with details, needing to know the precise age of the property, the dimensions of the garden in yards, the quality of the wood used for the kitchen cupboards, the annual cost of the central heating and the rates, and much more, which after a while began to rattle Alex. Showing strangers round her home was intrusion enough without the relentless questionnaire. Her veiled displeasure finally got through to Mr Peterson, who whispered testily to his mother, 'Put a lid on it, eh, Ma?'

For Alex the final straw came when they entered the one room she would have given anything to pass by. The corner bedroom. It wasn't a large room at best, but it shrank still further with four adults gathered about the bed that had been Alaric's. The bed she'd sat upon so often since his death, moping, remembering, sobbing. And here she was, trying to be cheerful when strangers commented on it, as if nothing had happened.

'Might do for Joe,' the wife said.

Mr Peterson sniffed dismissively. 'Not enough room for his gadgets.'

'Could be a guest room.'

'For one small guest maybe. How about you?' he asked his mother.

She shuddered. 'No, thank you. It's got an atmosphere. And I wouldn't want to see that river every time I looked out.'

Alex sprang to the door. 'Let me show you the Box Room!'

The June flooding, which she made no mention of until it could be avoided no longer, caused dismay all round.

'The garden was flooded?' said the wife. 'The entire garden?'

'Yes, but only for a week or so.'

'Does that sort of thing occur very often?'

'Oh no. Never before in all the time we've been here, and not for decades before that.'

Mr Peterson took over. Until now he'd been content

to follow the women around and merely chip in every so often.

'If it happened once, it might happen again.' Alex conceded that anything was possible. 'You could raise the bank,' he suggested.

'We could, but I imagine it would be terribly expensive.'

'Yes, but it'd keep the water out.'

'It would also change the look of the garden. We might not be able to see the river from the ground any more.'

'So you'd rather risk further flooding.'

'Yes. Would you like to see the garage?'

She showed them the inside of the garage, which wasn't really worth seeing, told them that there was a fair amount of storage space at the top of the narrow staircase, then walked them round the grounds to a fresh barrage of questions from the sparrow-woman – about the plants, the fruit trees, the type of grass, the chances of getting a good gardener locally.

'That old oak doesn't look too fit,' Mr Peterson opined in the south garden.

'It's diseased,' Alex said. 'Have to come down sooner or later.'

She just wanted them to go now. She knew that the prospect of further flooding had put them off, if nothing else had. It was only as they were about to leave that Mr Peterson let slip that he was a risk assessor for an insurance company. Alex couldn't help a chirrup of laughter.

'Well, no doubt you've assessed the risks here then.'

He smiled tautly, and the three of them climbed into their silver-grey Xsara Picasso. She watched their departure with relief. Turning towards the house she looked about, as she had done when showing them round, hoping to see Mr Knight pottering somewhere. Was it one of his days? She wasn't sure – reliable as he was, he was rarely predictable – but she could have done with his company right now.

10: 43

Alaric's first thought was to take a backward step, hopefully to the willow and his reality. His second was to look a bit further. He spotted what might have been the beginnings of a path, but as it ran straight into prickly scrub he cast about for something more promising. He was still looking when he heard voices and the thrashing of leaves, the crunch of dry twigs. Far from ready to meet strangers in an unfamiliar reality, he stole away as quietly as he could. Not quietly enough, however.

'Whassat?'

'What's what?'

'I heard something. Must be her.'

'Could be some animal.'

'Could be, might not.'

'We could do with the meat if it is.'

'I could do with her meat more. This way.'

'Why don't we spread out?'

'You spread out, I'm going down here – if it's OK with you, Cap?'

'Yeah, go on. If you find her save some for me.'

Once the voices had died, the only sounds were the small ones he himself made as he forged a complicated path between multitudinous trunks, and bushes so spiky and dishevelled that they were virtually impassable. But unlike Naia, who had chosen a different direction when she began her exploration, he found his way out of the forest quickly, if no less suddenly. With the way so dense he was unprepared for an early end to it, and pulled up only just in time. One more step and he'd have dropped into water.

He stood on the bank of a river that looked like a broad band of liquid rust, across from which a further belt of very tousled woodland stretched as far as he could see in either direction. The water, which smelt at least as rank as the forest, was strewn with large

107

thunder-green lily-pads with frayed, upturned rims. But it was the silence that struck him most of all. He'd thought the forest quiet, but out here, beyond its precincts, there wasn't a hint of sound – and everything was so still. In spite of the abundance of vegetation it looked and felt as if nothing breathed here.

This observation was moderated by a factor of one when a small black shape rose from the trees across the river, wings frisking madly as it prepared to launch itself. When it was ready, the bird shot up for several hundred yards, straight as an arrow, to stop abruptly at a certain point, as though to assess its situation or position, before plunging back into the trees – a descent that ended with a single harsh cry, after which the silence and stillness returned, embellished by the interruption.

After the gloom of the forest Alaric welcomed the unshaded daylight, though it was a very inferior light, of a dirty yellow hue. But something about the sway of the river, the lie of the land, bothered him. He closed his eyes and pictured the view from his own riverbank; then, picture in place, opened them and saw how the essentials of that view corresponded with the fundamentals of this. This river was wider, and so much lower that it was hard to imagine it rising sufficiently to spill across the land, as his river had in June. Holding on to the emaciated trunk of a sickly-looking tree that sprouted from the overhang of the bank, he took in the stretch of water to his right. No distant stone bridge carrying traffic into and out of town. No town, he guessed. He peered the other way, to where, at home, a narrow pedestrian bridge arched, linking the Coneygeare to Withy Meadows. Again, no bridge. Differences indeed, but he was certain now that he stood on the bank below which, in his reality, a former soldier by the name of Eldon Charles Underwood had built a shelter for the small boat in which he wrote more than a hundred and fifty poems between the opening years of two world wars. The sprawl of the forest behind him suggested that it not only covered the area of ground where the garden should be, but the old cemetery, the school, the church, the village, perhaps the entire region.

Curious about this very alternative version of his world, he set off along the bank to where he estimated the landing stage should begin. There was no landing stage here, of course, but the flora ended abruptly, at a generous swathe of erratically-cut grass that sloped upward from the river, as a short flight of steps and more evenly-cut grass sloped at home. About to step into this open space he trod on something hard, a rusty-bladed sickle, which he might have picked up if not for the small imprecise sound that caused him to glance to his left; a glance that ended at the top of the rise, and the strangely-configured house glimpsed yesterday amid overlapping realities. Intrigued, he started towards it, but paused half-way. A black window stared out from the facing wall like a blank eye; any view from the other side of it would at present include him. He went on a little less boldly, and at the top crept warily to the nearest corner. He peered round. A man stood there. A stranger. Waiting for him.

'So good of you to call.'

A strong hand grabbed him by the shoulder, and before he could even try to wriggle free hauled him round the corner and along the front of the house. A door was flung back, and he after it, headlong into an unlit room, cracking a knee on the floor before sprawling on a skidding rug. The door banged shut. Bolts were rammed home. He rolled over, staring about him, and at the large man whose hunched demeanour in the subdued light suggested that he did not plan to offer him buttered scones and Earl Grey with a slice of lemon.

Ric had managed to shield himself from the worst of the assault, but his head throbbed, he could taste blood, and his ribs hurt like hell. Gus would have done much more damage if Scarry hadn't ordered him to stop, repeatedly, with increasingly angry insistence. When Gus finally stood up, only the 'Cap' mistook the flash of resentment for deference. No one asked Ric if he was OK, though Badger and Jonno cast sympathetic looks back at him as Scarry led them away, in Gus's twitching wake. Thus Ric was cast out, and Gus effectively promoted to second-in-command – though to an uninformed observer Gus would almost certainly have been taken for the leader, Scarry his bustling lieutenant.

In a coil of agony on the ground, the girl's face swam into Ric's mind. He'd never seen her before, he could swear he hadn't, yet there was something about her that wouldn't allow him to let Gus have his way with her. And she'd called him by his full name. The name no one knew here. She must be from the same place as him. From home. Maybe a girl from school he'd not noticed but who'd noticed him. There were things she might know, things he could have asked her given the chance. Like how to get back. But she'd gone. Seized her chance when Gus sprang at him. She wouldn't return. Wouldn't be that crazy. Which meant that his questions would find no answers and he would continue to be stuck here. And all because of that sod Gus.

There'd been a degree of camaraderie in the group till Gus arrived. Must have been about three weeks ago, a month at most. They'd been sitting round the fire that night, the small pale flames their only light. A fire was rarely needed for warmth here – if nothing else the climate was equable – but it was comforting to loll around, especially shrouded in the blankets Scarry had brought back with the air of a conquering hero one day. 'Inched 'em from the old geezer's,' he boasted. They hadn't asked how he'd managed it. It didn't matter. Having them was sufficient. There being only five blankets, there wasn't one for Gus when he turned up, but sometimes, after the first week, he was seen strutting about with one knotted round his neck, billowing behind him like a cloak, and you knew that that night he'd still have it and one of the lads would be feeling sorry for himself under a heap of leaves.

Gus's first appearance had been as dramatic as it was unexpected. He'd simply stepped out of the darkness, into their flickering circle, dropped to his haunches, all teeth and bonhomie. 'Hi. Gus O'Brien. And you are…?' They'd shared their food with him, little as it was, and over the next few days, ingratiating himself with Scarry, he'd become a fixture. Behind Scarry's back he was a different person, however, especially with the youngsters, slapping them round the head on a whim, thumping their shoulders with a fist, tripping them for a laugh. At first he would throw a grin Ric's way when he did something like this, expecting an amused response. Ric had made his disapproval plain once only, when Gus reached out and squeezed Jonno's balls when the boy was just standing there. Jonno's legs gave way. He fell to the ground, lay on his side, legs drawn up, hands between his thighs, unable even to groan.

'Why'd you do that?' Ric asked.

Gus grinned at him. 'Why'd you think?'

'He's just a kid.'

'Just a kid.' Gus's gaze returned to Jonno as if this hadn't occurred to him. A thin laugh. 'Hey, you're right, so he is.'

That was the moment he and Ric became enemies.

Little was known about any of them. Their former lives, friends, what sort of homes they'd come from. Discussion of such things was forbidden – an addendum to Scarry's no-moaning-about-loss rule: 'New place, clean slate,' he said. But however little was known about the others, nothing whatever was known about Gus. He volunteered no details, dropped no hints, so, there being nothing to go on, they took him at face value – not a comfortable assessment for any of them. Surprisingly, given his volatile nature, Gus made few public complaints about the world he'd stumbled into, or the rough living, the absence of every kind of luxury. He shared their sleeping space, hunted with them sometimes, bowed to Scarry's primacy, yet no one doubted for a minute that he was anything other than his own person. The nearest he came to group activity could be summed up in one of his more quotable invitations: 'Going for a wank. Anyone care to join me?'

Occasionally the six of them sallied forth to see if they could find an end to the forest, marking trees or breaking twigs to follow back, but it just went on and on in all directions but one: the river. There were no buildings, roads, footprints, any sign at all of recent civilisation. The only other person in the vicinity was the man from the weird house. The first time Ric saw him – on a ladder, fixing some of the slates on his roof – was with Scarry.

'Look at 'im,' Scarry whispered, parting the leaves at the edge of the clearing. 'Old twat.'

The man must have heard the voice if not the words, for he glanced their way, saw Scarry's face framed in the leaves, and waved. Scarry rushed Ric away without returning the greeting.

'He didn't seem unfriendly,' Ric said as they went.

'They never do at first. He'll turn, they always do.'

But even Scarry hadn't been too proud to accept the

provisions the man began leaving for them shortly after the kids arrived. Every few days they found a box of groceries on the wall beside the gate – things to cook and eat with too, and the matches that had made such a difference. Ric and the boys were thrilled to sink their teeth into real food for a change, and eat off plates, use forks, though none of it was good enough for Scarry. They returned the box each time under cover of darkness and it was refilled in a day or two, but never did they approach the man or his house. When Ric said that it might not be a bad idea if they thanked him for his kindness, Scarry sneered.

'No one does no one no feckin' favours. He's after summing.'

Ungrateful as he was, when the man disappeared for a few days every so often, Scarry was the first to complain when they had to go hunting for additional food. When he was absent for almost a fortnight, Scarry talked of knocking the house down. He didn't knock it down – it would have taken a bulldozer to do that – but he did try to break in: a vain ambition with that hefty padlock on the door, and windows both secure and unbreakable. He got the kids to help him kick a portion of the wall down instead, then personally stomped over the few decent flowers and the vegetable patch. Ric pointed out that they could have eaten some of the vegetables, but Scarry said the only veg he liked was the spuds they put in the fire, so leave 'em. He did like chicken, though, and ordered the seizure of three of the five hens pecking around the yard, along with all the eggs they could lay their hands on. He kept some of the eggs, but lobbed the rest at the windows. It further angered him that the hens had been left food and drink while he and the others had not, overlooking the fact that the hens dined on meal and grain distributed by a feed hopper, that their liquid sustenance came from their usual plastic water fount. The cats were also catered for, by different methods and devices. There were several cats, but the tortoiseshell was the only one that didn't scoot when approached. This was obviously the man's favourite. They'd seen him petting it while merely feeding the rest.

Perhaps because he was of a different generation, or because he had a roof over his head and they didn't, when Gus joined them he developed an immediate antipathy towards the man, beside which Scarry's paled. The killing of the tortoiseshell cat was a deliberate strike against him. Only Gus and Scarry had partaken of the cat's flesh that night. The boys had eaten nothing, crouching silently together at the outer edge of the firelight. Ric had nibbled a squirrel haunch for a few minutes before also losing his appetite. While they were tucking in, Gus said: 'I'd like to see *him* on a spit.'

'Who?' Scarry asked.

A nod in the direction of the house. 'Or maybe his head on a spike. Yeah, that'd be good. Shove an apple in his trap – if there were any apples in this crap-hole.'

'What's he done to you?' Ric asked.

Gus turned to him. 'Why, soft spot for him, Priscilla?'

Ric had not responded to this and the subject had been dropped, but some days later, beaten and abandoned in the forest, he realised that Gus was capable of carrying out any threat, indulging any dark desire, for no other reason than that it amused him.

12: 43

The interior of the building Alaric had been hurled into was a fair match for its exterior. There was a very unfinished air about it, with the boulders and rocks intruding significantly at several points. The furnishings were not much more sophisticated – a sagging old armchair beside a rough stone fireplace, a couple of rickety cupboards, a plain pine table under one of the windows, with a pair of equally plain chairs. On the table stood a typewriter that belonged in a museum. Several unlit oil lamps were placed more or less strategically, and over to one side there was an untidy kitchen area with a small stove. Unremarkable ornaments were lodged on many of the walls' protrusions, along with a number of framed photographs, prints and drawings. The walls being far too uneven to allow shelving, books – a great many books – were piled wherever there was floor space. Also on the floor were three colourful rugs, one of which Alaric sat upon, more worried about what was going on than he cared to admit.

'Stay put or I'll flatten you.'

He stayed put. His captor began pacing the room, fists clenched, darting furious glances at him as he stalked this way and that.

'I would have helped you,' he growled. 'I *did* help you, dammit. I left provisions for you and you accepted them. I left blankets by the gate, you took them. I didn't get any thanks, but I didn't do it for thanks. You were lost, scared no doubt, glad of anything you could get. I understood that. But then you stole from me. Even that I could forgive, food's not laid on here, but you trampled my garden too, my vegetables, which are very hard to raise here these days, took my chickens, smashed part of my wall. What had I done to deserve such treatment? But even that was nothing compared to what you did to my cat. You burned him. You stripped the flesh away. You hung the remains on my door to taunt me. That I will *not* forgive! You'll get nothing out of me now except...'

He broke off. Ceased his pacing. His eyes, having adapted to the feeble light seeping in the window panels, saw what they'd missed before, even outside. He stepped closer; bent to examine Alaric's face.

'Have I made a mistake?'

Alaric glared back at him. 'Bloody right you have.'

'You'd better get up. Chair over there.'

He got to his feet and went to the armchair by the unlit fire. Aldous U retreated to the table. Sat on a corner of it, one leg dangling.

'How long have you been in this reality?'

The question surprised him almost as much as the attack that had ended with his sitting here. But there was no point in pretending he didn't understand it.

'About half an hour. Bit longer maybe.'

'Your first visit, or...?'

'First. And last.'

'How did you come upon this house?'

'I was down by the river. I just...saw it.'

'Have you visited many realities?'

'This is my fourth. Apart from my own.'

This evidently surprised his host. 'Your fourth? Well now.' He paused. 'Is your mother alive?'

'What?'

'I'm trying to place you. Is she?'

'No.' Hard to admit, even after all this time.

'Does the name Kate Faraday mean anything?'

'She lives with us. What is all this?'

'And do you know someone called Naia?'

'Look, before I answer any more qu—'

'I see that you do. When did you last see her?'

'Just before I came here. But—'

'Where? Your reality, hers, some other?'

Alaric sighed; gave up. 'Mine. She seemed to think it was hers until Kate came along.'

'She didn't expect Kate to be there?'

'Don't know. But she shot off after that.'

His inquisitor relaxed. Became more agreeable. Noticing Alaric massaging the knee he'd fallen on when flung into the room, he said, 'Sorry if I hurt you. Bit edgy today.'

'A bit! Can I go now?'

'Well, you *can*, but isn't there anything you'd like to ask me?'

'I just want out of here. I don't like being treated this way.'

'I have apologised. But there's the door.'

Alaric got up and went to it; bent to draw the first of the two bolts.

'The way back is along a path which starts about

ten paces to the left of the gate,' Aldous U told him. 'You'll have to poke about a bit, it's pretty well concealed. Old habit. If you'd met some of the people I have, you'd want to cover your tracks too.'

'How long have you lived here?' Alaric asked, drawing the other bolt.

'Seven years, give or take. Not much longer, though. It's fading fast.'

'What is?'

'This reality. I say fading, but it might end with an almighty clatter, or some other way. The ways a reality can expire are rarely predictable.'

'I didn't know realities could just *end*,' Alaric said, straightening up.

'With experience of just five there'll be quite a bit you don't know.'

'There are a lot, then.'

Aldous U smiled. 'A fair few.'

'Are all of them...normal?'

'Define normal.'

'I mean do they all have people in them?'

'This one doesn't. Apart from we incomers, of course.'

'But the others?'

'I haven't visited them all. I couldn't possibly visit them all, no one could.'

'Because there are so many.'

'Mm.'

'The ones you have, though. Are there people in all of them?'

'There are physical differences here and there, but I'm sure they all think of themselves as people,' AU said. 'There are no talking mice or armoured bears if that's what you're wondering – unless they were on a break the day I strolled in.'

Feeling that he was being mocked, Alaric changed the subject.

'Where will you go when you leave here?'

'Back to my original reality. And a proper Withern Rise.'

'A "proper" Withern Rise?'

Aldous U left the table and went to the door. Alaric stepped aside to allow him to open it; was beckoned outside to look at a plaque on the wall. He stared.

'You call *this* Withern Rise?'

'Why not? The position's right.'

They went back inside. Alaric remained by the door while AU seated himself on the chair at the typewriter end of the table.

'Did you build this yourself?' Alaric asked, meaning the house.

'Myself? The size of some of those stones? No, it

was already here. There was no lock on the door – I only started to feel in need of security a couple of months ago – but all the essentials were in place: the bed, the stove, this table, the chairs, many of the books, and a very handy toilet, the like of which I've not found anywhere else. There was a note on the table. "It's all yours," it said. "But watch the sky." So I moved in and have been watching the sky ever since.'

'Why watch the sky?'

'For signs of decrepitude. As the eye mirrors the soul, the sky quite often reflects the health of the reality. It certainly does here. This is a "fast" reality, evolving many times more rapidly than most. It would take several millennia for a standard reality to age as much as this one has in seven years.'

'The note you found,' Alaric said. 'Was it signed?'

'No. But I knew the handwriting.'

'Whose was it?'

'Mine.'

'Yours!'

'It's a long story, and not entirely my own.'

Not being in the mood for long stories, Alaric returned to an earlier subject, which interested him far more.

'This Withern Rise you plan to move to…'

'What about it?'

'Do you own it?'

'Not yet. But I expect to.'

'Who lives there now?'

'An Alex and an Ivan,' said Aldous U.

'Naia's parents?'

'Not exactly. These days.'

'These days?'

'Never mind. The point is, they're selling and I hope to buy.'

'Won't it be a bit pricey?'

'For someone who lives in such squalor, you mean?' AU grinned. 'I'm not as impoverished as I might seem. Over time I've accumulated substantial funds thanks to some realities being a little behind others, a day here, a day there: a few dropped seconds per year over aeons, perhaps. Just enough time-differential for me to see where the markets have gone in a reality that's a fraction ahead and capitalise on the information in one or more of the laggers. I've spread my profits across several realities so as not to arouse suspicion and can gather them to me whenever I wish. I could have made much more, become very wealthy indeed, but I have no heirs, and my requirements are few. I realised quite recently that all I've ever really wanted, materially, was my own Withern Rise. Why don't you come and sit down? I think we know by now that we're not enemies.'

Alaric took the chair at the opposite end of the table. 'Do all realities but this have a proper Withern Rise?' he asked.

'Not all. But most.'

'And is there always an Alaric or a Naia in those that do?'

'Only in those to which the family returned in 1963. Other families occupy the rest.'

'I went to one yesterday where there were no Underwoods,' Alaric said. 'This woman rattling around there on her own. Just her and her lousy dog. Garden was a bomb site. Crummy old fences instead of brick walls.'

This caught AU's interest. 'Fences. There aren't many with fences.'

He got up and went to one of the cupboards, at which he knelt to remove a large green book, rather like a Victorian moneylender's ledger. Kneeling there, turning the pages, he asked Alaric if he'd gone to the village of that reality. Alaric said that he had.

'Spot anything unusual?'

'You mean like too-tall buildings, triple green lines instead of double yellows, traffic driving on the wrong side of the road?'

'Yes, that sort of thing.'

'And the shop,' Alaric said.

'Which shop?'

'Mr and Mrs Paine's.'

'What was wrong with it?'

'No Mr and Mrs Paine.'

AU stopped leafing. 'Did you notice a different poster on the wall?'

'Yeah. Some man in a suit.'

'No queen?'

'There was nothing about his private life.'

The book slammed shut. 'Reality seventy-eight. It's one of the few in which the British monarchy is appreciably different.'

'Reality seventy-eight?' Alaric said. 'The realities are *numbered*?'

AU returned the ledger to the cupboard. 'Yes. By me.'

'And there are seventy-eight?'

'Oh, there are more than seventy-eight. Many, *many* more.' He resumed his seat. 'Would you like to hear how the monarchy of R78 turned out so differently?'

'I'd rather hear how many realities there are.'

'In the fifteenth century England of that reality,' AU said anyway, 'it was proved conclusively that Edward Plantagenet, eldest son of Richard, Duke of York – next in line to the throne – was the progeny not of the Duke and his lady wife but of the lady wife and a common archer by the name of Blaybourne. This ruled Edward out of the succession, so that when the cuckolded Duke copped it in battle (along with his second son, Edmund) it was his third son, George, who took up the succession, and George's descendants who ruled henceforward. That bloodline produced a King Rupert for the seventeenth century and two Henrys for the eighteenth. There was no nineteenth century Queen Victoria, but a queen of that name reigned from 1959 to 2001. In all realities but seventy-eight, the man who's now King there (your man in a suit) is a children's book editor in New York called Steve.'

'How do you remember all this?' Alaric asked.

'I remember it because I'm fascinated by alternative histories. But I suspect that you're not.'

'I've never been big on history.'

'Even the alternative kind?'

'Still too much like school. Why do you number the realities?'

'As a way of telling them apart, why d'you think? There are many variables of the Underwood See, some of which are worth visiting, some well worth keeping out of. I like to keep tabs on them.'

'The Underwood See?'

'You must have heard of it.'

'I'm not sure.'

'Bishop Underwood, founder of Withern Rise?'

'Yes, him I've heard of.'

'Naughty old lad,' AU said with relish. 'Put it about all over the place. But his misdemeanours caught up with him in the end and he was obliged to resign his office and retreat to the modest riverside estate he'd created for himself and his family some years earlier.'

'Withern Rise.'

'Yes. A "see", as I'm sure you know, is a precisely-defined district under the authority of a bishop or archbishop. His diocese. Just what our favourite Lothario no longer had once he chucked the job. The locals, presumably seeing a chance to rub it in, wasted no time in dubbing his property the Underwood See, it being all that he retained any jurisdiction over. What none of them knew – maybe it wasn't even the case back then – is that the garden of Withern Rise contains intermittent crossing points to alternative versions of itself. I've found eight there over the years.'

'Eight?' Alaric said. 'There are eight ways into other realities from Withern Rise?'

'I said eight over the years. None have been permanent fixtures.'

'And they're always around trees, are they, these crossing points?'

'Trees? Whatever gave you that idea? They're in the ground. The earth.'

'The earth! But…'

'But?'

'When I first met Naia I thought we'd been brought together by an ornament our mums had made from a piece of the Family Tree. I was wrong then.'

'Not necessarily.'

'But you said—'

'If a tree stands in a piece of active ground, the power, for want of a better word, could seep into the roots and from there through the rest of it. It's an attractive notion. I wouldn't discount it.'

'Why do some parts of the ground become crossing points and not others?'

AU leant forward. 'You wouldn't care to hear my pet theory on that, would you?' Alaric gave a non-committal shrug, which it pleased AU to take for intense interest. 'Sounds a tad loony-fringe even to me,' he said, 'but I believe that the Underwood See hosts a chance confusion of shifting ley lines (or some sort of equivalent; for convenience's sake let's call them ley lines) and when the lines intersect, as they do every once in a while, we find crossing points to realities where identical intersections have simultaneously occurred.'

'What do you mean by "shifting" ley lines?' Alaric asked.

'They move about under the surface, infinitely slowly. Sometimes they stop moving altogether, for months or years. That's when we get our crossing points. When the lines move on, the crossing point ceases to be. A new one forms soon enough as a rule, but an extended break between the termination of one and the formation of another can leave you stranded for quite a while. Before the latest one opened last December—'

'Under the willow in the north garden?'

A perfunctory nod. '– I was stuck here for eighteen months. Tedious times, I can tell you. So? What do you think?'

'Of what?'

'My shifting ley lines.'

'Like you said, it's only a theory.'

AU sat back, disappointed that the first outing of his hypothesis had met with such indifference.

'Naia had a theory,' Alaric said, 'that we crossed into one another's realities because certain factors, as she called them, all came together at the same time.'

His host smiled. 'Another nice idea. I've found a way to pass between realities that suits me, but I'm sure there are others.'

'If you can go to any reality, why live in this one?'

'Oh, it wasn't always like this,' AU said. 'When I first

130

came here it was very different. There was more visible life – not human life, but fascinating birds and insects, interesting species of mammal – and there were flowers everywhere, glorious flowers, and the skies were blue, the river was higher, the water clear. As the one place I could return to and know that my presence would not influence events, it was hard to beat.'

'But you can visit any reality you want?'

AU unclipped a black leather wallet from his belt, from which he took a small grey pouch. He placed the pouch between them on the table.

'Whenever I happen upon a reality for the first time I bring something of it back with me, something natural: a handful of leaves, fragment of bark, a smattering of earth. If I wish to return at a later date I take a pouch like this (which by then contains some of that material) and as long as I'm at a crossing point I'm there in a single step. Material from one reality has no place in another, so when it gets a chance to go home it will, taking the carrier along for the ride.'

'How long did it take you to work that out?'

'Not as long as you might think. This took rather longer.' AU tapped the wallet. 'Whenever I want to return from a reality I put its pouch in one of these, go to the crossing point, and back I come. It's made of leather, you see. Tanned animal-hide acts as a barrier between a reality and any unadulterated material that belongs to it. I was rather chuffed when I discovered that.'

'These pouches,' Alaric said, 'do they come in different colours?'

'Why, thinking of marketing them?'

'Just wondering.'

'I make them out of odd scraps that I happen to have about. The colours mean nothing.'

Alaric tugged the green pouch from his pocket. Surprised to see it, AU took it from him.

'Where did you get this?'

'I thought Naia dropped it. Tried to go after her to give it back, ended up here. Now I know why. It wasn't hers.'

'Oh, but it was. On loan. It brought her here. I intended to meet her, but she came early. Not a wise move as it turned out, but that explains how you came to be here. Until now I assumed it was by chance.'

'How was she able to leave here if she didn't have one of those leather things to put the pouch in?'

'This is an easy reality to depart these days,' Aldous U said. 'It still draws its natural material to it, but it can no longer hold it if the carrier is at the crossing point. I've tested this personally.'

'Any idea what brought Naia to my reality?'

'Not yet. Where were you when you met?'

'In the north garden.'

'By the willow?'

'Yeah. We sort of crashed into one another.'

'Then it was you.'

'Me?'

'Naias and Alarics are essentially the same person. Even if you'd never met a Naia you might be vaguely aware of one now and again, in dreams or perhaps as an unseen presence. But you have met, and a link has been forged which can be reactivated in the right circumstances. The circumstance this time was that you were at the very point she was about to return to in her almost identical reality. Your being there pulled her off course.'

'All right, I get that,' Alaric said, 'but if she went back to her reality from mine…'

'How could she if she didn't have a pouch containing material from it?'

'Well, yes.'

'Her clothes,' said Aldous U.

'Her *clothes*?'

'She was drawn to your reality by your presence in just the right spot, but she would have continued on to hers when you were no longer physically close, courtesy of the natural fibres in her garments. I only wear things

133

made from synthetic fibres when I set out from here. Not being natural, they have no home reality.'

'So how do you get back?'

AU displayed the green pouch on his palm. 'By way of an R43. Never go anywhere without one.'

'Does the number mean anything?' Alaric asked.

'Year of my birth. 1943. Keeps me grounded.'

'Can you give me some idea how many realities there are?'

'Some idea is the best I can do. I've personally visited thousands—'

'Thousands!'

'—but that's just a drop in the ocean. Realities spring up all the time. Click, there's a new one, blink, another dozen, each one complete to the last dentist, taxi driver, overpaid footballer, suicide bomber, grain of sand.'

'How can you know all this? How can you *possibly* know all this?'

'Much of what I might tell you about the realities,' said Aldous U, 'is informed by over forty years' experience among them, but a lot of it's guesswork, so take what you want from anything I say and jettison the rest. There are more questions than answers in the reality multiverse, and few rules. Just as you think you've got it all buttoned down you see something, or something happens, which sends you spinning right back to square one. But this much I do know. The great majority of realities are very short-lived – I mean *very* short-lived – but that still leaves unquantifiable numbers of all-singing, all-dancing, fully-populated realities rich in history and calamity, each one set to create limitless spin-offs with variable futures at the drop of a hat, with or without apparent reason. As life generates life, reality fosters reality. We're all clones of clones of clones, developing in different ways, responding to stimuli of every kind and variety. Very little that you see, hear or sense in your home reality is wholly original.'

'Doesn't sound like there's much room for God in all this,' Alaric said.

'God? Don't make me laugh.' He laughed anyway. 'You might as well believe in reincarnation, fate, destiny, or imagine there's some meaning to life. There's no meaning, there's no divine plan, no glorious heavenly paradise full of dead relatives where we swan about for all eternity doing sweet bugger-all while managing not to be bored out of our skulls listening to harps. We're born, we live out our pitiful little lives, we're scattered on the roses, end of story. Care for a Darjeeling?'

'I'd rather know your name.'

'My name? Why?'

'Seems fair. You know who I am.'

'If you insist.' AU gave his preferred name, in the form he considered appropriate in the present company.

'Naia mentioned you,' Alaric said. 'Why the U?'

'It's the initial of my surname.'

'As in Underwood?'

AU smiled. 'As in whatever you like.'

'Why not the whole name? Sound pretentious, just the initial.'

'I know.' He twinkled. 'I wrestle with that sometimes.'

'So what are you? Some sort of relative?'

'Of yours? I'm not sure people from different realities can be related. If they were, everyone would be swamped with surplus uncles, aunts, cousins, and what-have-yous. People would have to take three jobs to pay for all the Christmas and birthday presents.'

'Naia said you leave notes for her. Why? What's in them?'

'They're my way of…easing her into things. Reality things.'

'Why her? I mean why that Naia if she's not the only one?'

'Why her? She's the victim of a devastating quirk of chance, in spite of which she remains cheerful,

136

intuitive, compassionate – and she was born in the same reality as me.'

'You come from the same reality as her?'

'Her original reality, yes. I—'

He would have said more had something not thumped the window. They both craned forward, but whatever it was had already dropped from sight. There was no question as to where it had come from, however. The gangling youth in cowboy boots standing in the yard with his hands on his hips was so surprised to see two faces looking out instead of the one he'd expected that his eyes popped.

'Now he *has* to be one of them!' AU growled, jumping up. His chair clattered to the floor behind him. He stormed to the door, and out.

Alaric heard little of the ensuing conversation. Conducted across the yard, it started quietly enough, but when the youth unzipped his jeans and urinated on the one beautiful flower there, the turquoise iridian imported a week ago from R216, Aldous U howled with fury and rushed at him. The youth whooped derisively, hopped over the wall, and ran into the forest shouting abuse. AU, preferring the gate, went after him.

Alaric glanced at his watch. That package for his father. If he wasn't there to sign for it, Dad would go ballistic – 'Can't trust you to do a damn thing, can I? One hour, just one sodding hour out of your busy schedule, that's all I asked.' Frustrated, because there was still so much to learn here, he looked for the green pouch that would bring him back whenever he wished. It wasn't there. The only pouch on the table was the grey one from the leather wallet. It being all there was, he grabbed it. He started for the door, but before he reached it remembered what Aldous U had said about unshielded pouches taking the bearer to the reality its contents belonged to. He returned for the wallet, put the pouch into it, sealed it, and went out.

Beyond the gate he turned left as advised and, after a little foraging some way along, found the path. It wasn't easy to follow, being both convoluted and overgrown, but eventually he came to a familiar part of the forest, where a single step returned him to the willow in the north garden.

His willow, his garden.

13: 39

It wasn't until she was approaching the house after leaving Alaric's reality that Naia missed the pouch that had taken her to Aldous U's. Furious with herself for losing it, she stomped around the garden for some twenty minutes before calming down, and did little with the rest of her day but walk and sit on her own pondering the events of the morning and their relation to a certain other episode that had changed things so dramatically eight months ago. First, the two Alarics. She'd barely glimpsed the one who saved her from that reptile, but from what she had seen he wasn't much less of a savage himself, in appearance at least. And the second one, in the reality she'd mistaken for her own, he remembered her from February but not from June. He had not met young Aldous, or seven-year-old Rayner. What was that all about? What it was about, she decided after sifting through a range of possibilities, was that in February, at the instant she was flung into this reality, all exits barred to her, a new reality had splurged into existence to allow Alaric to take her place in her original *and* carry on in his. In that fateful instant one Alaric had become two. But if that had happened wouldn't it mean that there was also another Naia, at a Withern Rise in which her mother still lived? If so, it could mean that the Naia she'd seen walking along the hall yesterday was herself as she would be if she was still in her true reality. As she *was*, there. Taking this supposition even further, it seemed possible that the other Naia had turned the kitchen tap in that reality just as she herself was about to turn it in this. Their realities were so close in all but one respect that there'd been a freak seven-second unification of (of all things) the two taps.

There were other conundrums that she couldn't begin to solve on her own. The Alaric in the woods for one. More information was needed about him before she could factor him into the equation. It would probably help if she had someone to talk to about all this. A brainstorming session with the right person might produce theories and solutions that eluded her in her solitude. But there was no one.

Or was there? Wasn't there one person who might hear her out and not think she should be sectioned? Someone she was going to Cambridge with tomorrow because they had agreed a week ago that they needed a day away from Eynesford and the house?

14: 43

Mid-evening found Ric squatting in the dark of the forest, way beyond the flickering light that illuminated the faces of the five sitting around the fire. The talk he overheard was mainly Scarry's and Gus's, with the latter's sharp voice dominant. The young boys were plainly terrified of Gus now, and even Scarry was careful not to push him too far. It was obvious to Ric, listening from the dark, that it was just a matter of time before Scarry was displaced. When that happened the youngsters would become Gus's whipping boys, thumped and cudgelled for the smallest misdeed or wrong word, or just because he felt like it.

What they were saying was not of great interest until Gus's 'About time we saw to him' caught his ear, followed by Scarry's quizzical 'Howja mean?' Ric saw Gus draw a finger across his throat. After that, all he could hear was the occasional crack of wood, fracturing like snapped bones.

FLASH 3

The tank was too low to risk. She'd meant to top it up after leaving that wretched restaurant, but the frantic head-down splash to the car had washed the intention from her mind. She pulled in at a filling station, hauled her bulk once again out of the car, and inserted the nozzle in the tank, huddling over it like a witch at a cauldron because the roof was too high to shelter her from the slanting rain.

'You all right, love?' A man at the sliding window of the shop.

All right? Are you kidding? I'm unattached and world-beatingly pregnant, I'm wet, I'm cold, and I have no idea what sort of life I'll have from this point on, or if I'm doing the right thing for my child.

'Fine, thanks.'

She replaced the pump, secured the cap, hurried

into the shop. 'Not much of a night,' the man said, and she said, 'No, not much,' paid, and returned to her vehicle, where she yanked the belt across her inflated stomach and rejoined the motorway.

Gradually, over the next twenty minutes, the rain eased off. She was within ten miles of her destination when two things happened almost simultaneously. The first, by a small margin, was the appearance in her headlights of the first sign for Stone; the second, a sharp kick down below. She placed a hand on her belly: 'Two possibilities,' she said to the bump. 'Either you know you're going home and are getting excited, or you're taking it out on me for making you be born there rather than someplace else, which might set your little tootsies on a brighter road.'

She went with the first of these without much difficulty, and suddenly everything was all right. By the time she reached Stone, and saw the sign for Eynesford, she was all warm and fuzzy inside.

Part Three

A POLICY OF INDIFFERENCE

1: 39

She found Kate in the south garden, chatting with Aldous.

'You about ready?'

Kate said that she was, but almost squashed The Plan flat before it had a chance to worm its way into any conversation by asking Aldous if he was sure he didn't want to join them. Fortunately, he was not tempted.

'Cambridge? Not me. I've never been that far.'

'You have. The nursing home up north.'

'That doesn't count.'

'Oh, come on, lad, spread your wings a little.'

'My wings'll get by unspread,' he said, and ambled away, kicking leaves.

The walk to the bus stop in the market square took about fifteen minutes. Knowing that buses to Cambridge were fairly frequent, they hadn't bothered to look up the times, and ran like mad things when they saw one about to pull away. Puffed, they climbed the stairs to the top deck, where Kate cried: 'Front seat's empty!'

They flew to the front, jostled for hip space, then leant forward to gaze at the world beyond the wide smeared window above the driver's cab like a pair of excited children to whom even Stone High Street seemed interesting from such a vantage point. Once on the Cambridge road, the town behind them, they settled back, and communication dwindled to sporadic bursts of chatter and occasional giggles over nothing much. As the journey progressed, Naia's thoughts turned to the plan to take Kate into her confidence. Where could she start? She'd acquired her knowledge of other realities bit by bit, and even now, living in one herself, was struggling with the latest information; but Kate, unaware of any of it, would have to gulp the whole lot in one hard-to-swallow lump. How would she take the news that she had a duplicate a mere step away? That her life, her history, her every thought perhaps, was replicated elsewhere?

It was Kate's first visit to Cambridge and she wanted to see all the highlights without having much idea what most of them were. At every turn she exhorted

Naia to take pictures, and Naia obliged, keen to use the Canon PowerShot she'd been presented with on her birthday. Driven by Kate's desire to see as much as possible in the time available, everything was observed and recorded in haste: the reaching turrets and spires; the teetering clock towers; the archways, quadrangles and landscaped gardens; the warm red brick of some buildings, the cool medieval stone of others; the leaning Tudor houses casting shadows over tributaries; the tiny courtyards defended by hydrangeas; cats drowsing on walls; the little pastry shops and delicatessens; the bikes chained to railings – and all of it, the whole city, canopied by a beefy blue sky spattered with timid splurges of white. Kate was very taken with the rows of varnished punts on the quay opposite Magdalene College – 'Waiting for punters?' she said, pleased with that – and two other punts, occupied this time, propelled by standing young men with the arms of sweaters around their necks, passing beneath the grey weather-beaten timbers of the Mathematical Bridge at Queens'.

'It's just too picture-postcard for words,' Kate said of this last.

'They work at it,' Naia said.

Kate arched an eyebrow. 'When did you get so cynical?'

'It's a teenage-angst thing.'

With all this rushing from site to sight there was no time for chat about anything of substance beyond the place, the experience, the day. Lunch – warm baguettes bulging with chicken and salad – was bought at Peppercorns in Rose Crescent and devoured on a bench in Petty Cury, where a handsome young violinist in torn jeans made Naia blush as he serenaded them with Vivaldi. All morning, and through lunch, Naia hoped they'd be able to find some quiet place and an hour to themselves for what she wanted to say, but the odds in favour of this did not improve until Kate spotted a noticeboard propped up against the petite Knights Templar church at the junction of Reinald Street and Confraternity Walk, opposite Charleston College: an invitation to step inside and, for a small fee, make a brass-rubbing.

'Can we?'

'Why not?'

There were over a hundred brasses to choose from. Varying in size from as small as a table-mat to around two yards in height or length, they were facsimiles taken, for the most part, from the tombs of Tudor dignitaries, medieval knights and ladies, and colourful, if less noble, characters of note or interest. Kate chose a medium-sized John of Gaunt, Naia a plump friar with a lascivious grin. Apart from the two elderly ladies who had issued them with the requisite materials, they were alone within those grey stone arches and high stained-glass windows. Perching themselves on wooden stools across from one another at a baize-covered table, they bent over their work, and silence descended at last. In a minute or two, Naia broached, quietly, nervously, the subject of the day. The year.

'Kate…'

'Ye-es?'

'Ever think about reality?'

'Reality?'

'The world we know. Live in.'

'Oh, this is going to be rubbish. Why did I choose a man? They're always difficult.'

'I mean do you ever wonder if there's anything more than what we see about us?'

'About us?'

'Or beyond us.'

'If you mean as in heaven, this is just the place to muse on it.'

'Not heaven. Just, you know, if there are other versions of things. This building. The world. People.'

'Mm.'

'Mm what?'

'Do you think I should have done this in gold rather than silver?'

'The silver's fine. I mean do you wonder sometimes

what reality is?'

'Is it all a dream, you mean?' Kate said.

'No. I mean if our reality's the only one.'

'Oh, now he's got a broken nose!'

Naia tried again. 'What would you say if I told you I'm not from this reality?'

'Umm...?'

'If I said I didn't belong here.'

'I'd probably say...oh, that's better...I'd probably say what are you doing here making brass-rubbings with me then?'

'I'm serious,' Naia said.

Kate looked at her. 'Is this a philosophical discussion?'

'Sort of. For now.'

'Good. Had me worried there for a sec.'

Kate went back to her work. Naia waited. Nothing else came.

'Aren't you going to ask me to explain?'

'Explain?'

'About me not belonging to this reality.'

'Yeah, course, explain away.'

She set aside her stick of copper-coloured wax. There was only one way. Rush at it, as they'd been rushing all day. Deal with the astonishment and questions when it was all out.

'I was born in a reality just like this,' she began. 'Except there I didn't have an Aunt Liney and Mum's still alive and you're still in Newcastle, with a boyfriend, and—'

Kate glanced up. 'Boyfriend?'

'And that's where I should be right now. Not Newcastle, at that other Withern Rise with Mum and Dad.'

'*Boyfriend*?'

She forced herself to slow down. 'In this reality,' she said, more evenly, 'there was no Naia until February. Alex and Ivan had a son, not a daughter. The son was called Alaric. But something happened the day you came to live at Withern. Just before you arrived. We switched realities, Alaric and me, and I've been here ever since. I'm stuck here and he's stuck in mine, with my mum, and...' She sighed. 'God, I miss her.'

Kate continued with her work, much more slowly than before.

'That's nothing against you,' Naia went on. 'In an ideal world I'd have you too, but...well I feel cheated. My mum and dad don't remember me, any more than this reality's Ivan remembers having a son. And now there's another Alaric. His reality's just like this. Well, I don't know about Cambridge, but the garden's exactly like ours, so the house probably is too, and the village, everything. There's even another you there.'

Again Kate looked up. 'Another me?'

'She's living with that reality's Ivan, as you're living with this one's. Sounds mad, I know, but that's the way it is, in a nutshell.' She beamed. It was out at last. Shared. 'I've told you. Phew! What a relief.'

Kate dropped her stick of wax and reached across the table; touched the back of Naia's hand. Her eyes were moist.

'Oh, my darling. It must be so hard for you.'

'Well, yes…' she admitted, mildly puzzled.

'I wish there was something I could do.'

'Yeah, but that's it,' Naia said. 'That's the trouble. There's nothing anyone can do. I just needed to talk about it. It gets pretty lonely, keeping it all in.'

'It will get better,' Kate assured her. 'I promise it will, in time. The loss might never quite go away, but you must try to move on. Oh, that's so *trite*. Forgive me. I'm hopeless. I don't know what else to say.'

Her chair scraped noisily on the stone floor as she stood up, near to tears that she needed to stem in private. She almost scampered to the old oak door. As it groaned to behind her, the women at the desk looked at Naia. She avoided their eyes. Stared at the two unfinished brass-rubbings, then at the hand Kate had touched. The smudge of silver on the back of it.

154

Alaric's day was very different to Naia's. About half-way through the morning he saw, through the kitchen window, Lenny Paine and Paul Kearley ambling along the path from the side gate. He went to the front door, but on opening it saw not one view of the garden but many, one upon the other, appearing and supplanted as briskly as dealt playing-cards. In some views, identical in all major details – position, dimensions, colours – strangers chatted or worked; in one he saw a greenhouse; in another a pagoda; in a third a small blue tent under the Family Tree. One garden boasted a paved concourse with a swimming pool in which children and a dog swam.

'What's with you?' Len said as he and Paul approached.

'Dazzled,' Alaric managed as the many views shivered back to one. 'By the company,' he added when Paul glanced at the sky.

It being the autumn break from school, they were under no obligation to use their time well, so they headed for the open spaces of Withy Meadows to pass some of it in aimless pursuits. Even before they reached the long bridge Len and Paul were saying how bored they were, with life, being under their parents' thumbs, living in a place where nothing happened. Pretending equal disenchantment, Alaric, mooching silently for the most part, was free to wonder what the glimpses from the doorstep might signify, and returned time and again to a worry born of information that Aldous U had imparted in his home in the malodorous forest.

When they reached the Climbing Wall in the south-west quadrant of the Meadows, they clambered up, around and over it, but Alaric, still distracted, missed his footing too often for the others to ignore – until one jibe too many sent him scrambling after them threatening violence. He stayed with Len and Paul for most of the day, jumping on and off benches, hurling stones and cans, being loud and coarse, eyeing up girls he didn't fancy, all of which served the useful purpose of suppressing the fears that would return when he was alone again, and keep him awake half the long night.

3: 39

Within moments of waking to the leisurely beat of powerful wings, Naia was at her window watching a pair of swans career along the river, just above the surface. She remained there for some time after they had resumed a more sedate course, on the water, her view embellished by the glint of a spider's threads at the top left corner of the frame. No sun yet this side of the house, but a creamy haze over all, and such a tender stillness now the swans were quiet, until a mallard burst from a clump of reeds and skidded half the water's breadth. She glanced back at her bed, tempted, then again out of the window, and decided that she could sleep any time, that days like this were precious, in any reality.

As she stepped into her pants, she noticed in the vertical wall mirror that the red strikes of fingernails were still visible on her stomach. Shuddering at the thought of what nearly happened that day, she jumped into her clothes, tugged a brush through her hair, and crept downstairs. In the kitchen she took a gulp of orange juice from the fridge and, at the front door, slipped into a warm coat and her everyday shoes. Beside her shoes were two pairs of Ivan's and the scuffed brogues Kate had worn to Cambridge. The sight of these returned her to the misunderstanding at the brass-rubbing centre. During the journey home she had assured Kate that she hadn't been referring to Alex, was not still in mourning, and Kate had accepted this, or pretended to, while neglecting to ask what she *had* meant. Without such an invitation Naia knew that she must continue to keep the whole reality thing to herself.

She unbolted the door as quietly as she could, wincing at the rasp of metal withdrawing from metal, and on the step closed it with care, failing to anticipate the thud it always made at the last, whatever you did. But then she was out, tasting the white mist that rolled across the lawns, obscured the greater boundaries, veiled the cemetery wall. She loved the benevolent claustrophobia of these gardens in autumn. With no idea what to do now she was outside, she decided on a general tour, starting at the south garden. Ideally such a circuit would begin at the landing stage, but that would take her near Aldous's willow, and he might hear her and call out. She didn't want company just now, even his.

But Aldous remained in her mind as she set off across the lawn. If ever anyone had been dealt a poor hand it was him, whisked from childhood in the middle of one century to old age in the early years of another. The boy inside, who'd so recently shinned up trees here, run and jumped and yelled, sung at the top of his voice, had no place in the body of a seventy-one-year-old. He saw the world through the eyes of a child – he must do – but went out of his way not to let it show that he was so much younger than he looked. Aldous had developed an excellent line in sage nodding, and platitudes that must have sprung from the lips of his parents or grandparents, and when he thought himself observed he slowed as he walked, stooping a little. It was admirable in a way, but very sad.

Of the things he did to pass the time, Aldous most enjoyed jigsaws, fishing and reading. The jigsaws were mainly relics of previous generations (often with a piece or two missing, like the generations themselves) brought to him from the attic or the box room. Sometimes, at weekends or on fine evenings during the summer, Naia had worked on these with him, at a table on the lawn. He usually fished in solitude, however, from the landing stage. He'd caught a number of fish, which Kate had prepared and cooked for him – for all of them when the catch was big enough. A month ago, he hooked a large tench, and was proud of himself because it had put up such a fight. It was on the barbecue three hours after he delivered it, when even Ivan, who generally avoided the lodger in the garden, toasted his efforts.

In spite of his love of stories, Aldous refused to join the library or cross the threshold of Stone's only bookshop, a small well-stocked independent, so his reading matter, like the jigsaws, was brought to him. With an eye more on his pleasure than his education,

Naia sought out books of a kind a boy of the 1940s might have enjoyed. Kate helped in this, with rather more knowledge than Naia, though she herself was a child of the '60s and '70s. Many of the books they brought home were not to his taste, but others thrilled him. Reaching the finale of a 1930s translation of Pinocchio, he said to Kate, who happened to be nearby at the time, 'I'm like him the other way round,' and did a turn around the garden, walking stiffly for her benefit.

He also relished *The Arthur Rackham Fairy Book* (especially the gorier drawings from *Jack the Giant-Killer*), *The Arabian Nights* (though he described the politically correct 1990s retelling they brought him as 'soft'), and *Swallows and Amazons*, recalled all too well because his mother had been reading it to him and Mimi just before the flood in which his childhood ended. Picking up the narrative of the Ransome six decades on, he heard his mother's voice, read the characters' names with her accent. He also enjoyed *Perrault's Tales of Mother Goose*, which Maman had read to him and Ursula when he was nine and Ursula eight. Mimi and Ray had been considered too young for some of those. There'd been no pictures in Marie's volume, and Aldous was so taken with the luminous Dulac illustrations in the library edition that Kate and Naia bought him a copy to keep.

Something that pleased Naia as much as anything about Aldous's return after such an absence was that her cat took to him straight away and was often seen accompanying him round the garden. Once, she'd come upon Aldous lying on his front on the lawn reading aloud from one of his story books – to the cat, who sat at his elbow, listening intently. She was fondly recalling this scene when she paused at the Family Tree to dip a hand in the message hole. Not really expecting to find anything there this early in the day she was surprised to come up with an envelope – an ordinary brown envelope, not the usual wax-sealed hand-made kind – with a trimmed piece of paper inside, and printed on the paper, in pen:

> So SORRY ABOUT WHAT HAPPENED. IF YOU WOULD CARE TO TRY AGAIN, COME THURSDAY, 3PM. THERE'LL BE ANOTHER POUCH AT THE WILLOW FOR YOU. DON'T LOSE THIS ONE PLEASE - AND FOR YOUR OWN SAFETY DON'T BE EARLY!
>
> IN HASTE, AU

Thursday. Today. The envelope was slightly damp. Must have been there all night. She returned the note to the envelope and folded it, stuck it in her back pocket, and went to the willow in the north garden. There was no pouch in the ivy around the trunk. She imagined that he planned to slip into the garden and put one there as close to the designated time as possible so she wouldn't be tempted to defy his instruction a second time and come early.

She went back to the house. It was going to be a long day.

4: 47

Alaric woke convinced, where yesterday he'd been merely concerned, that his reality would end very soon. In the bleary drift to full wakefulness his first thoughts were for himself, but then less selfish considerations crept in, such as, if this reality was about to end, shouldn't he warn people? Which brought a whole raft of quandaries and contradictions. Would warning them do them any favours? It wasn't as if he could save them, after all. He had that grey pouch, though. Maybe he could use it to get Dad and Kate out. But there was a downside to that too. If there was a Withern Rise in the reality the pouch took them to, and an Ivan and Kate in residence – or an Alex who hadn't died – they would hardly be welcomed with open arms. They might be taken for con-artists, or lunatics. They'd be homeless. They wouldn't have bank accounts, social security numbers, tax codes, all the rest of it. They wouldn't officially exist. How would they even get *by* there? Of course, he could still go. He would adjust somehow. But he couldn't come back and check that everything really had ended. Well he *could*, but what might he find? Total blackness, an airless vacuum, instant death? No, if he had to go alone, he couldn't return. Ever.

Ah, but what if he didn't leave and this reality didn't end, and everything just carried on the way it was? He wasn't a great student, he had few ambitions, no bright-eyed career goals to work towards. He was nothing here. Felt like nothing most of the time. There was always this unsettling buzz in the back of his mind that seemed to be saying, 'What are you going to do with your life?' This brought guilt. What *could* he do? He wasn't like his mother. She'd been so inventive, so innovative, resourceful, so keen to put things into the world that could not have been made by anyone else. If he'd only inherited a fraction of her ingenuity, creativity, zest. As things stood, all he would be able to add to the world – and even this wasn't a foregone conclusion – would be a child or two, but he felt distaste for the part he would have to play in such an enterprise. Of late he'd even become uncomfortable with his friends' graphic sex talk. It didn't used to bother him – he used to participate, enjoy it – but these days when he joined in it was an act. What was wrong with him? Just a phase? Some sort of belated reaction to his mother's death? What if it wasn't either of these? What if he didn't grow out of it or get over it? Who was to say this wasn't the real him emerging from adolescence? If that was it, what kind of life was he going to have? A life of pretence; making out he was something he wasn't, that he—

He swore, stuffed his head under the pillow, tried to go back to sleep.

5: 39

After such an early start, and with so many hours to squander till mid-afternoon, Naia's morning crawled. She passed a portion of it within the lee of the hawthorn hedge, in a faded deckchair whose old wooden frame creaked and wobbled at the slightest movement, from where she hoped to catch Aldous U sneaking to the willow with the pouch he intended to leave for her. The wait gave her time to speculate about his place on an alternative family tree. Exploring several scenarios that might have added another Aldous to the Underwood line, she was drawn to one in particular.

Suppose her great-grandfather, AE Underwood, had been struck down by some fatal illness, or killed in an accident, in the mid or late 1920s. If he'd died around that time he wouldn't have met and married Marie Montagnier, there would have been no Grandpa Rayner to father Ivan, and consequently no Naia or Alaric. Had AE dropped out of the picture that early, his sister, Larissa May, would have taken ownership of Withern Rise. According to her mother's researches, in 1927 Larissa gave birth to a son, Edwin, who (as she'd had nothing more to do with his father from the point of conception) had been given the Underwood name. In both of Naia's realities, Edwin had never lived at Withern, or, as far as she knew, anywhere much less than two hundred miles away. Her grandparents, in both realities, had lost contact with Edwin's branch of the family, so she had no idea if he had fathered children of his own; but an Edwin who had grown up at Withern (in the new scenario) and inherited it from his mother upon her death would almost certainly have had a different partner to an Edwin who'd spent his life in Dorset. Different partner, different children – one of whom might have been called Aldous and think of Withern Rise as home. A pleasing dénouement, she thought, but not a likely one. If such an Aldous existed why wasn't he still living there instead of in a sickly-looking forest in an outlandish hovel that he *called* Withern Rise?

Growing chilly in the hedge's lengthening shadow,

she gave up her vigil at last and went out by the side gate. Still needing to kill time, she sauntered to town, loitered in a couple of shops, and, after a while, crossed the river to Withy Meadows, where she approached the little boating lake. Until a few weeks before, there were boats and canoes on the lake, but the season was over and they'd been taken in. There were still a lot of ducks about – there were always ducks here – but also a number of geese and swans, strutting along the banks looking hungry. The geese ignored her, but one of the larger swans padded towards her, wings flaring. She backed away and found an alternative route, round the far side of the closed café.

She started across the Meadows, sometimes on one of the winding paths, sometimes the grass, avoiding other strollers and keeping well away from the unruly scatters of kids unleashed on the world for half-term. Spotting a group of lads, fourteen- or fifteen-year-olds, swaggering in her general direction, she swerved away, not looking back in case they took the glance for an invitation. Only when she'd put what she hoped was a safe distance between herself and them did she turn to check on them. They were at the boating lake, trying to outface the unfriendly swans.

Reaching the river some way downstream from Withern Rise, near the long bridge, she wondered where else she might go to pass the time, and could think of nowhere. Beside the bridge lay a heap of bikes whose young owners were not in evidence until she was about to cross it, when they ran out from some mischief under it, yelling and laughing at whatever they'd done, disentangled their bikes, and shoved past her in their eagerness to get to the other side. Deflected, she changed her mind about crossing the bridge and wandered along the bank, flopping, with a bored sigh, on a flaking wooden bench. There, with nothing new to feed her imagination, she quickly ceased to notice the sounds of everyday: the whistles and cheeps of unseen birds, the sputter of a biplane in the crisp blue sky, the weary chug of a distant goods-train. The slightly sleazy smell of the water also receded, taking with it the tang of woodsmoke from the Coneygeare allotments. Only when a small boat slid from the trees that obscured the house from her bench did she stir. There were two men and a boy in the boat, fishing idly as it drifted. When one of the men hailed her, she returned the wave and, back in the here-and-now, headed homeward.

There certainly didn't seem to be a shortage of people interested in the house. The latest viewers were a building contractor and his wife, and their three teenage children. Why do they always come in families as if on an outing? Alex wondered, switching on her best 'I'm so happy to conduct guided tours of my home for total strangers' smile. But these, like the others, seemed pleasant enough. The man, smartly dressed and perky, introduced himself as, 'Feathering, call me Harry,' and the children were bright and polite and the woman very complimentary about every room they were shown into. Alex was rather taken with them until she overheard Harry whispering to his wife while she herself lingered in the hall to give them some time to themselves. 'Just the job, Jilly,' he said. 'We can hive off a third of the land on that side for four houses, six if we really pack 'em in, put up a wall between us and them, and still have more space than we need. If we lop all those trees along the drive we could really open the place out, and we could sink a pool where that crap veggie patch is, get ourselves a motor cruiser for the river, put up a summer house… Jesus, can't you *see* it?'

An offer – the full asking price – came in via the

estate agent's an hour after the Featherings' departure. Alex texted Ivan, who phoned a few minutes later.

'That's great, Lex. Call the agent and accept, will you?'

'I don't want to accept,' she said.

'Eh? You think they'll go higher?'

'I don't care how high they go, they're not having Withern.'

'What?'

'They want to partition the garden, build houses, put in a swimming pool, all sorts of things.'

'Do what they like once they own it,' he reminded her.

'They're not going to own it.'

'Alex. Come on. We can't turn offers like this down just because we don't like what the buyers want to do with the place.'

'I can.'

Pause. Then: 'It is in my name, you know.'

She hung up.

She was sitting on one of the pews in the back porch when Mr Knight found her.

''Lo, Alex. Glad I bumped into you, I wanted to ask about...Alex?'

The eyes that turned to him were flooded.

'I'm not good company today, John.'

He leant into the porch. 'What happened to your hand?'

There was blood on her knuckles. 'I've been abusing the wood.' She slapped the seat with her open palm. 'Nearest I could get to a punchbag.'

He entered the porch. Sat down opposite her. 'I'm intrigued.'

She told him about the Featherings, their plans for the property, Ivan's comment before she disconnected.

'I've never hung up on him before, but I'm so mad that he *said* that.'

'Or mad that it's true?' Mr Knight said gently.

'What are you,' she said, 'my therapist all of a sudden?'

But it was said lightly. There was something about this man that calmed her. Warmed her. She knew what it was. He liked her. Simple as that. He liked her. No ulterior motive. She wasn't sure how rare that was, but it touched her.

'Do you think I should just do as I'm told and accept their offer and be done with the place?'

'I'm not sure I'm the one to advise you on this,' he said.

'But you have an opinion. I know you have an opinion.'

'Well, if it were me...'

'Yes? If it were you?'

'I might hang on a bit. These are early days and already you're getting top offers. The right purchaser could well turn up before long.'

'That's what I think. But Ivan might have phoned the agent to accept that rotten offer. If he has, I'll never forgive him.'

'You'll forgive him, Alex.'

'I don't want just *anyone* living here,' she said hotly. 'This is where my son spent his entire life. I have photos of him here from when he was a day old. We recorded his every year, in all seasons, while he grew, changed, developed. I sat at his bedside, reading to him at night, holding his hand when he was unwell. I walked him to school through many icy winters, attended so many Parents' Evenings, helped him with his homework, encouraged him in anything he wanted to try. I watched telly with him, cooked for him, shouted at him sometimes. I hit him once, you know.'

'Did you?'

'Slapped his face for some smart-aleck remark. I'll never forget the look in his eyes. Disappointment. I never did anything like that again, though I'm sure he deserved it often enough. He wasn't always easy to live with. Moody as hell the last couple of years. We lost the closeness we had when he was younger. But I tried to give him space. Isn't that what mothers are supposed to do for their growing boys? Gave him too much space in the end.'

Mr Knight reached out. 'You didn't know it was going to happen. No one could have.'

She gripped his hand in both of hers. 'If I'd made more effort he might not have wanted to be alone so much. I might have been with him that day and he'd still be here, and we wouldn't be selling, and I wouldn't be hating Ivan.'

'You don't hate Ivan.'

'Right now I do. "It is in my name, you know." How could he say that to me? How could he *say* that?'

The tears burst from her. Mr Knight put her head on his shoulder while she sobbed her misery away.

7: 43

The air stank, the forest stank, everything stank, and it was getting worse by the day. They moaned about it, cursed it, tried to focus on something else, but there was little else, so Scarry decided that they would go fishing, in the stinking river. The three lads grumbled quietly, but did not speak out. Gus did, though.

'I'd rather go hunting.'

'We haven't done so well hunting lately,' Scarry said.

'Yeah, well maybe if we all went out together we'd catch more.'

'Another time. Today we fish.'

Gus's head went back. He gazed vacantly at Scarry's puggish face. Then that ludicrously wide smile of his crept slowly into place.

'Sure, Cap. Worrever you say.'

Scarry's idea of fishing was standing in the shallows with cones formed from the tough lily-pads. When the fish swam into the cones they were whipped out of the water and tossed onto the bank to gasp and flap until the life left them. This was a method he himself had recently devised, and he was rather proud of it. The one time he tried it, a few days ago, he brought home a single fish, not a very large one, but he believed that if they applied themselves as a group they would be rewarded with a more substantial haul.

It took some effort, but they managed to yank six lily-pads from their thick stalks. Shaping them, they spread out across the river. The brown water reached the youngsters' waists and Scarry and Gus's upper thighs and smelt even worse now they were in it, but they leant forward with anticipation – an anticipation that quickly faded when no fish could be persuaded into the cones. They remained in place for about thirty minutes before Gus lost patience and threw his cone away. 'Stuff this for a caper,' he snarled, and climbed out, pulled his boots on, and stomped into the forest. Meaningful looks were exchanged, but no words.

In a while Gus happened upon two specimens of a species of rabbit that he'd seen once before but failed to catch: round-eared, orange-furred creatures with stunted forelegs and blunt claws. Presumably male and female, these two were in the process of mating, so engrossed – or poorly tuned to danger – that they were easy prey. He delivered such a blow to the topmost skull with a stout piece of wood that the creature underneath was also stunned. He snatched them up by their hind legs, the female's still kicking feebly until he scattered her brains on a tree. He started back then, double prize in hand, mood much improved.

At the river some minutes later, Scarry conceded defeat and gave the word to jack it in. He made for the bank, intending to throw his bulk onto it and sprawl in the grass for a bit before rising. It was a fateful case of unfortunate timing. Lurching rather than climbing out of the water, his shoulder struck Gus's knee as he emerged from the trees. Gus's leg gave way. His head jerked back, cracked against a trunk; his arms flew out. The pair of rabbits soared away, sank into the river.

It was a combination of things that did it for Gus; the triple shock of being unexpectedly barged into, banging his head, and losing the rabbits he'd been looking forward to showing off. The last shred of the control he'd maintained with such difficulty since stepping into this miserable world evaporated in a heartbeat. He reached for the throat of the lumpen fool he'd been obliged to defer to these past weeks and leapt into the river with him, scattering Jonno and Hag before they could clamber out. He thrust Scarry's head under, settled a boot-heel on his chest, and kept him there. The two boys spluttered to their feet, Jonno wailing with fear, while Hag made the mistake of tugging at Gus's sleeve, hoping to persuade him to release the thrashing Scarry. Gus was not to be persuaded. He flattened Hag's nose with his fist. The boy sank into the water, which ferried him into the reeds, where he remained, face down. Jonno bleated in disbelief.

'Shut it, you!'

When Jonno didn't shut it, Gus reached for him, gathered a fistful of hair, and snapped his neck. He then picked the body up and threw it onto the bank.

'Anything you wanna say?' This to Badger, still in the water, a little downstream, backing away.

'No, n-nothing.'

He scrambled for the side, hoping to escape, but Gus's passion was now so extreme that every movement aggravated him. He removed his foot from the now motionless, staring Scarry and jumped up the bank. Badger was easy to catch. At least as easy as the copulating rabbits.

8: 47/36

The thought of kicking his heels while his reality ticked second by second towards extinction made Alaric edgy. He opened the leather wallet and took out the grey pouch. The pouch bore the number thirty-six. What sort of reality might that be? But did it matter what sort so long as it wasn't this one? He put the pouch in his pocket, clipped the wallet to his belt, and went to the willow in the north garden. He counted down from five before taking the step past the trunk. The disorientation was so mild this time that he thought he might have imagined it, especially as the tree looked no different at all. But, remembering that it had looked the same in the reality with the Alsatian, he returned the pouch to the wallet and parted the leaves cautiously. The north garden looked just as it should but for one detail. To his left, just beyond the spread of the willow, stood a small tool-shed. There was no such shed at home.

He stepped clear of the tree. If the garden was this much like his, it seemed probable that a variation of his own family lived here. Naia's reality? Could be. His heart thumped. If it was her reality, her mother would be here. The nights he'd dreamed of seeing *her* again!

The hedge this side of the garage provided adequate cover from the windows of the house, but there would be no warning before someone came round it, as Kate had yesterday at home. Rather than risk a difficult meeting with someone he knew very well but who didn't know him, he started towards the river. Trees lined the bank all the way to the landing stage. He would approach the house trunk by trunk until he could get a clear view of it, and hopefully of one or more of the people who lived there. He'd got no further than the second tree, however, when an oath caused him to spin round. Back at the willow, Aldous U was waving frantically at him. In his non-waving hand he carried a large bunch of purple flowers.

'It is you, isn't it?' Alaric said, retracing his steps.

'Keep your voice down,' Aldous U whispered. 'Who the hell do you think it is?'

'I mean who I met yesterday.'

'Again, who the hell do you think?'

'You might have been this reality's version.'

'I'm both this reality's version and the one you met yesterday.'

'Oh, is this the Withern you plan to buy then?'

'*Hope* to buy. A good offer's come in, might've missed my chance.' He slapped the wallet on Alaric's belt. 'I thought I made it clear that I don't appreciate being robbed. Maybe my first assessment of you wasn't so far out after all.'

'I only borrowed it,' Alaric said.

'And how would you have got it back to me? By post? Well, never mind that now. Got to get you away from here.'

He put the flowers out of sight within the willow, led the way to the path along the north wall – concealed by fruit trees and bushes – and to the side gate. Out in the lane, he steered Alaric to the left.

'If anyone appears and I tell you to go,' he said, 'you shoot off without a word, understand? And hide your face. No one must see you. No one, you hear?'

'I hear, but—'

'Wait. Talk in a minute.'

The lane ended abruptly some yards short of the river, at which point a narrower path veered off to pass the bowling green and the municipal tennis courts, wend nonchalantly through a small copse, and conclude at a single-file pedestrian bridge over a tributary: the

Marina Bridge as it was known, though the marina was a good stone's throw along. They did not get as far as the bridge, however, for AU rushed Alaric into the copse, intent on putting a number of trees between them and the path. They stopped a little back from the bank, below which cruisers and houseboats were moored, on the corner where the tributary met the main river. Alaric demanded to know what this was all about.

'It's about you not being seen here,' Aldous U replied.

'So you said. What you didn't say was why.'

He didn't say now either, but nodded towards the marina, packed with gleaming boats beyond the sheltering trees.

'Your great-grandfather had a boat-yard there back in the thirties and forties.'

'Not my great-grandfather,' Alaric said.

'There was an Alaric Eldon here too.'

'Yeah, well I'm more interested in today.'

'Yes, I remember. Not big on history.'

'Look, I need to know something. Need to know if my reality's going to end.'

AU looked at him. 'What makes you think I'd know?'

'You're more likely to than anyone else. Are there any…you know…signs to look for? Apart from the sky, I mean. The sky looks OK.'

'What sort of signs?'

'That's what I'm asking you.'

AU returned his gaze to the boats. 'The most common indication that a reality's nearing its end is a glut of those "Acts of God" insurance folk wisely decline to bet against. Flash floods, tidal waves, earthquakes, category-five hurricanes, that sort of thing.'

'Sounds a bit close to home,' Alaric said.

'I'm sure it does, but most realities survive such excesses – just.'

'How do I know mine's chances?'

'Same way anyone else does. You wait and see.'

'Will I know if it's about to end, though?'

'Possibly, possibly not.'

'You're a big help.'

'I'm not all-knowing and I'm no fortune-teller,' Aldous U said. 'There aren't always overt indications anyway. Any reality can snuff it at any time, with little or no warning.'

'Just as well that's not common knowledge,' Alaric grunted.

'Yes. Be a lot of very jittery people about if it were.'

'What about my glimpses?'

'Glimpses?'

'Didn't I mention them?'

'I don't think so.'

'Well, I'm just sitting, or I open the door, and suddenly

I'm looking at people or things that shouldn't be there. The other day I saw your house.'

'My house in R43?'

'Yes.'

'Well, impromptu peeks into neighbouring realities aren't uncommon,' AU said blandly.

'They aren't?'

An almost curt shake of the head. 'They all occupy the same space, and every so often a fault occurs, briefly revealing a small part of one to another. Most go unnoticed because the majority of realities are so alike. Sometimes we glimpse buildings, sometimes bits of terrain, sometimes people. What do you think ghosts are?'

'Ghosts?'

'Ghouls in corridors, spectral figures at the end of the bed, they're not displaced or malevolent phantoms. They're individuals going about their lives in their realities – no less spooked, I expect, by reciprocal sightings of us in ours.'

'What about the spirits of people who died a long time ago, seen in old houses, on staircases, at airfields and so on?'

AU waved a dismissive hand. 'Links occasionally form between small pockets of realities set apart in time, so that odd scenes from one age play over and over in another, like looped film. A more interesting anomaly, to me anyway, is the displacement of objects. That has long fascinated me. I suppose it's happened to you?'

'Not sure what you mean.'

'Small personal items – a keyring, say, a pencil sharpener, a spoon – they're not where you thought they were. Where are they?'

'You tell me.'

'Relocated momentarily to another reality. They usually bounce back in seconds or minutes, and we say, "But I looked there three times!", then forget about it. But sometimes things don't return. A shoe slips unnoticed from the foot of a sleeping child being wheeled along in a pushchair. A chance instant later, a fragment of that reality pulls apart and the shoe becomes tangible in a neighbouring one, where a passer-by sees it on the ground and pops it on a wall in case the mother comes back looking for it. If she does, she doesn't find it because the shoe's been moved in the other reality, become part of it – even if there's no corresponding child there to wear it.' He glanced at his watch. 'So much for planning. I expected to have finished here by three. It's not going to happen now.'

'What happens at three?' Alaric asked.

'I've arranged to meet Naia in R43.'

'What for?'

'To *meet* her. We haven't so far. Well, we have, but she

doesn't know it yet. Um…you wouldn't meet her for me, would you? Tell her I'm running late.' Taking his hesitation for acquiescence, AU said: 'Give me that pouch.'

Alaric handed over the grey pouch and AU tipped out a handful of leaves and a couple of withered flowers, then turned it inside out and shook it thoroughly before substituting half the material from a number 43 pouch in his wallet.

'Is that enough?' Alaric asked when the grey pouch was returned to him.

'Ample. I overcompensate. Stick it in your pocket, not the wallet, or you'll go home instead in those clothes.'

They returned to the garden, and the willow, under which AU detached a key from a ring on his belt.

'This fits the padlock on my front door. Meet Naia at the crossing point and take her to the house. Give her my apologies, tell her I won't be long, and make yourselves at home. And watch out for those lads.'

'Did you catch the one who peed on your plant?' Alaric enquired.

'No. Probably just as well, too.' He picked up the glorious bunch of flowers from Señora Fariña's exotic little shop in the Eynesford of Reality two-one-six. 'Either I'd have murdered him or he'd have murdered me. See you later!'

Last night had been a slaughterhouse – in his dreams. In the depths of the forest, curled up against one of the ancient flights of steps that led nowhere, he'd ground Gus's mean face into the earth, gouged his nasty little eyes out, beaten him to an oozing pulp. Over and over again he'd done this, with pleasure. The spirit of the dreams had stayed with him in the hours since, evolving into such a deep, dark anger that by early afternoon he had come to the conclusion that the only way to diffuse it was to eliminate the cause. He set off for Scarry's house. As he drew near, his foot struck a stone as big as his hand. He picked the stone up, and with it a vision of himself stepping into the arena: Gus starting towards him wearing that crazy grin of his, long arms dangling, ready to flip his fists up at the last, only to be thwarted by this stone, swung around from the hip, a great wide sweep that would end with the bastard's skull cracking like an egg.

Eager for this very satisfying finale, Ric approached the ruined house with stealth, but parting the leaves to assess the relative positions of those beyond, he found the one thing he hadn't bargained for. The site was deserted.

Deprived of the reckoning he craved, all desire for it drained away. He dropped the stone, retreated, and wandered aimlessly for a time, during which a more natural hunger replaced the need for violent retribution. When he came to the strange house in the clearing, he stopped. He'd never been here alone before. Once, during the period when food was regularly left for them, he and Scarry and young Badger had found the man in his yard, cutting back weeds and overgrown grass with a sickle. When the man saw him his jaw had dropped and he'd just stared. Ric might have approached and asked what was so shocking about his face, but Scarry had whisked him and Badger away before words could be exchanged.

The man wasn't there today. The padlock on the door proved that. Ric thought of the food that might lie beyond the door, but recalling Scarry's failure to gain entry that other time, he was surprised, on going round the back, to find a window off the latch. Hoisting himself over the wall, he opened it further. He looked inside, weighed his courage, and climbed into shadows.

10: 39/43

Naia had returned to the willow in the north garden around two-twenty to see if there was a pouch there yet. There was, and again it bore the number forty-three, though this time the fabric was pale blue. With so much time still to wait she loosened the cord at the neck of the pouch and looked inside. Finding that it contained nothing but leaves, grass and earth, her first thought was that she was being toyed with and she very nearly tipped the contents out in anger – but resisted, pulled the cord tight once more, and shoved the pouch into her pocket out of harm's way.

The idea that the phantom letter-writer was making a fool of her persisted, however, and rebellion set in. Wait till three just because he'd *told* her to? Ha! She went round the trunk, and, with thirty-seven minutes still to go, took the step which, in a single giddy moment, delivered her to the forest she'd left in such haste two days earlier. Rather than wait there for Aldous U, she decided to make her way to his house and startle him in his lair – an advantage she would milk mercilessly. She'd had enough of being manipulated. And just let those yobs try anything today! She snatched up a length of broken branch. Anything!

Having some idea of the direction this time, she began picking her way through the forest. The journey was no easier than previously and she made many a false turn, but eventually she reached the wall that enclosed the house, from where, to her great annoyance, she saw that the door was again padlocked.

11: 43

It was just after half-past-two when Alaric returned to Reality forty-three. He was at once oppressed by the gloom, the stench, the deathly silence, though the last of these was disturbed within a minute of his arrival by a distant drone that grew steadily more sonorous until a bumble bee the size of a child's fist swerved around a tree and narrowly missed his head before careering unsteadily on its way, as though it had imbibed too much of its favourite tipple.

If he'd known that Naia was already in that reality, he too would have gone straight to Aldous U's house, but he did not, and, wishing to be clear of the forest until he had to be there, he again made his way to the river. From the bank, the light, though an improvement on that which he'd put behind him, seemed even more jaded today, while the water smelt even more noxious. Obliged to put up with both the jaundiced light and the odour, he contented himself, while not being in any way content, with squatting on the bank and tossing pebbles onto lily-pads. The minutes crawled.

After so long, it felt strange to stand within fully-formed walls, beneath a ceiling not composed of branches and leaves. Savouring the experience, Ric glimpsed, through a partially-open door, the fundamental requisites of a bathroom. He pushed the door back and saw a lavatory with a spherical bowl decorated with small pink flowers. The novelty of having access to a toilet induced a desire to use it. He lifted the seat, which was of a spongy green material. There was no liquid in the bowl until he introduced some, wondering as he did so where the waste went. He was about to turn away, as he'd got used to doing from whatever tree or bush he'd used, when a couple of his mother's insistences kicked in. He put the seat down and looked for some sort of flushing device. There didn't seem to be one, but when he passed a hand across the manufacturer's logo – a small amber shield bearing the legend J Harington & Son, Suppliers of Jakes since 1596 – he heard a small rumble beneath the seat, and when he looked the bowl was empty again. He would have washed his hands then – the end to a perfect visit – but he saw nothing resembling a tap, so one of his mother's strict injunctions had to go by the by.

A rummage in the small kitchen area to one side of the main room turned up a few cans and packets of foodstuffs, all of which required cooking; but he cleared out a biscuit barrel, polished off the last of a stick of brittle French bread, and dipped into a cereal called Special T. There was a carton of goats' milk, but he gave this a miss, taking the cereal packet with him on what he intended to be a quick inspection of the last room – the bedroom – before taking his leave.

13: 43

Round the back of the house Naia found an open window. What an opportunity, she thought. When Aldous U returned, hopefully annoyed that she'd not been where he'd said at the hour he'd decreed, he would be even more disadvantaged to find her inside his house than if he'd merely opened the door to her. The thought pleased her.

She dropped the branch she'd carried through the forest and hoisted herself over the ledge.

14: 43

With at least fifteen minutes still to go, Alaric started along the bank, as he had on his previous visit. This time he had the key to the house. Maybe he would go in, poke about a bit before taking the path through the forest to meet Naia at the crossing point. If he was a bit late, well, serve her right for running out on him last time. Would she be surprised to find *him* stepping out from the trees!

15: 43

The room was just big enough to accommodate a single divan bed, a small side table, and a rail of jackets, trousers and shirts. Ric was about to leave when he noticed two framed photos beside the bed. He bent to peer at them. One was of a small child holding a multi-coloured plastic windmill, the other of an attractive woman in her thirties. It was the latter which brought a gasp. 'Mum!' He dropped the cereal packet; picked up the photo. It wasn't his mother, but the similarities were undeniable: the short fair hair, the amused mouth, the large bright eyes. He was still getting over this when he heard movement in the adjoining room. He returned the picture to the table, careful not to make a sound.

To Naia, it had the air of a temporary residence cobbled together by someone who cared little for comfort or the look of things. Apart from the way many of the rocks that made up the walls intruded into the room – and the several teetering piles of old books – it was all so much more ordinary than she might have expected of the domain of a mystery man from another reality. She quite liked two of the three rumpled rugs on the floor, which had an African look about them, but most of the other furnishings were very commonplace. Only two items caught her interest, both of them on the table under the main window. The first was a pouch like the one in her pocket, but a darker blue, with a tiny diamond pattern. Beside this there was a needle and thread and a small pair of scissors. The other thing of interest was the typewriter. *The* typewriter, obviously. Inspecting this battered relic, she was intrigued to see that the manufacturer's name, in large yellow letters above the platen, was Underwood.

'What are you doing here?'

She jumped round. A figure glared from the doorway of the adjoining room.

'Alaric!'

His scowl deepened, as if she'd insulted him. 'Ric!' he snapped.

'Ric...?'

There'd been no time during their previous encounter to study him. A more leisurely perusal did him no favours: hair tangled and greasy, face and neck unwashed, fingernails rimmed with dirt, badly chewed. His blue cotton shirt, very grubby, was two buttons short, one of the pockets of his black denim jacket was torn, and there were gaping holes in the knees of his stained and muddied jeans. He also had a bruise on his right cheek and a cut over one eye, but she knew how he'd acquired these.

'I don't imagine you live here,' she said to him.

His eyes did a scornful tour of the room. 'Live *here*?'

'Why are you here then? The owner a friend of yours?'

'Friend? I don't think so.'

'So you're here because...?'

'That's what I asked you.'

'And now I'm asking you,' she said, 'so how about an answer?'

Her confrontational manner had the desired effect.

'I'm...visiting,' he mumbled.

'Visiting! There's a padlock on the door.'

'The window was open. What about you? I didn't

hear the door, don't see a key.'

She hesitated before admitting that she'd come in the same way, adding: 'But I was invited.'

He smirked. 'Invited, and you came in the window?'

'I'm funny that way.'

'How do you know me?' he asked.

'If you need to ask that, then I don't.'

'You know my name.'

'I don't know anyone called Ric.'

'Here I'm Ric. At home I...' He stopped. Home: the forbidden subject.

'Where's home?' Naia enquired.

'Not here.'

She almost howled with frustration. 'God, you Alarics, you're all so bloody *difficult*!'

He frowned. 'All?'

Which she sidestepped. 'How long have you been in this reality?'

He screwed his eyes up, as though peering through fog. 'Reality?'

'This...place. Not all your life, I bet.'

'No, not all my life. I don't know. Months.'

'How did you get here?'

'No idea.'

'Describe how it happened, what you were doing.'

He thought back; something he tried not to do

these days. 'I was just sitting in the garden one day and—'

'The north garden, under the willow?'

'Yes. How—?'

'And next thing you knew you were here.'

'Yes! How do you *know* that?'

'It's the way it seems to work.'

'The way *what* works?'

'You really don't know what's going on, do you?'

'I wish I did,' he said, suddenly weary. 'And I don't know you, but...your face...'

'You probably have a better memory of the back of my head. I'd thank you for saving me,' she added, 'but I wouldn't have needed saving if you hadn't held my arms behind me.'

'I had to go along with that. I'm not proud of it.'

'Oh, that's all right then. For a minute there I thought—'

'Quiet.'

'What?'

'Quiet!'

She listened. Heard it. A key in the padlock. They turned towards the sound, one with the dread of the cornered intruder, the other with a thrill of anticipation.

The door opened. But—

'You?' Naia said. 'Here?'

Alaric jumped. He peered into the room, but couldn't make her out very well. He pushed the door further back. Daylight, such as it was, reached in and fell across her.

'What are you doing *here*?' he demanded.

'Seems to be the question of the day,' she said.

'Eh?'

Only when she angled a thumb at the room's other occupant did he see that she wasn't alone. From that realisation it was no stretch to equal the incredulity on the face of his gaunt and ragged mirror-image.

17: 36

Ivan rarely closed the shop early, but the town was dead today, so around mid-afternoon he flipped the notice on the door and locked up. In no great hurry to get back to the tense atmosphere at home he went the long way, through the village rather than over the Marina Bridge and along the river path. Even dawdling, pausing at the occasional shop window, it took him little more than twenty minutes to reach the side gate. He strolled round the kitchen garden and was just approaching the front door when Mr Knight came out and bid him good afternoon.

'Bye, John – and thank you!' Alex called from the kitchen, mistaking the greeting for another farewell.

Ivan nodded curtly at the gardener and went indoors. He had never taken the time to get to know Mr Knight, but in recent months had found him in close conversation with Alex so often that he'd started to wonder about the man's intentions. The one time he'd asked Alex what they talked about she'd replied, 'Oh, you know…things,' which spoke so many volumes, and so few, that he thought it best to leave it at that. Today, finding her arranging a vase of large purple flowers on the kitchen table, he jumped to the first obvious conclusion.

'Oh, flowers now, is it?'

She looked up, surprised to see him. 'Half day?' she asked.

He grunted. 'Town's deserted. Just twiddling my thumbs there.'

She returned to her task, smiling. These days, a smiling Alex was almost as rare as flowers in the house.

'Aren't they exquisite?' she said.

'Yeah, lovely, what did he want?'

'Who?'

'Who? How many visitors have you had today?'

'Ivan…'

He flicked the switch of the kettle, almost viciously. 'What?'

'You haven't accepted the Featherings' offer, have you?'

'Going to, soon as I've had a cuppa.'

'Well you don't need to now.'

'I think I do. We might not get another top offer for months, if ever.'

'We've had another offer. A better one.'

'A better one? Better than the asking price?'

'Much.'

He sat down at the table; asked for details. When she gave them he said: 'You're kidding me. *That* much more? You're sure you heard right?'

'Yes. I asked him to repeat it.'

'Jesus. But...why?'

'He says it's worth it to him. And he's a cash buyer, no chain, no house to sell, exchange contracts as soon as we're ready but to take as long as we need. It couldn't be more perfect.'

'It's too perfect.'

'How can it be too perfect?' Alex said.

'Where would someone like him get such a sum?'

'What do you mean, "someone like him"?'

'What do you think I mean? How do you know he's good for it?'

'I know because he told me.'

'And you believed him.'

'He said he's been investing successfully all his life and has never had much use for his profits till now. Why should I question that? He really wants this place. As it is. He won't be sinking a swimming pool, paving over flower beds, uprooting trees – or building houses on the land.'

'He might have some other kind of agenda,' Ivan said.

Alex bridled. 'Agenda! It might be news to you, but some people are actually what they appear to be. I'm telling you, Ivan, don't you dare – I mean don't you *dare* – accept that other offer.'

She picked up the vase of glorious flowers and swept out of the kitchen.

Ivan remained seated, staring at nothing, tea unmade. It was an exceptional offer, way above the estate agent's target figure, yet he was unable to welcome it, or even quite believe it, largely because of the cosy conversation he imagined Alex and Mr Knight had had at this very table just before he came in; a conversation in which the pros and cons of the offer had almost certainly been discussed in detail, and approved, before he himself had even learned of it. He felt conspired against. Withern was his home, his family home, built by *his* ancestor, not Alex's, certainly not Mr Knight's. How dare they discuss the disposal of it as if it were nothing to do with him?

It would take Ivan a while to get over the collusion of his wife and the garden help, but the sale of Withern Rise would go ahead, and fourteen weeks from the day of the offer removal vans would load up in the drive and head for their new home, a fine three-storey town house in a good part of Brighton. Five months after that, Ivan would begin an affair with Lili Tulloch, a television features producer who bore more than a passing resemblance to Kate Faraday.

Ivan and Alex Underwood separated on the fifth of October 2006, which would have been, or so they believed, their late son's eighteenth birthday. They were wrong about this, of course. It was actually the eighteenth birthday of the daughter neither of them could remember – alive and well in another reality entirely.

18: 43

Once she had confirmed that he was the one she'd met under the willow in his north garden, and not yet another, Naia said: 'Alaric, meet Ric.'

'Ric?'

'He seems to prefer it.'

Ric was still gawping at him with astonishment. 'I saw you before,' he said in a flat voice. 'You disappeared.'

'So did you.'

Ill at ease in the presence of this grungy version of himself, Alaric crossed the room and perched on the arm of the fireside chair.

Ric turned to Naia. 'Why does he look so much like me?'

'He is you,' she told him.

'What?'

'So am I, in a way.'

'What!'

'That's why I seem so familiar to you.'

'I don't *understand*!' he wailed.

Naia pulled one of the chairs out from the table and sat down on it; reached round the typewriter for the patterned pouch.

'Imagine alternative versions of everything you know,' she said with the world-weariness of one who's gone over this far too many times. 'That there's another you somewhere, another house exactly like yours, another...well, you name it. Can you do that?'

'Don't talk down to me,' Ric snapped.

'Sorry.' She dropped the pouch. 'I'm assuming in your case, but if I'm right, the three of us are from slightly different versions of the same reality. We all have, or had, the same parents, were born at the same instant, share many of the same memories. And all three of us came here via our willows in our north gardens. Does that...' she hesitated, not wanting to risk further condescension '...make sense?'

He did not reply, but went to the door; leant there with his back to the room trying to apply all this to his own experience. While he attempted it, Naia again asked Alaric what he was doing there.

'I was asked to come.'

'By?'

'The person who lives here.'

'I thought you didn't know him.'

'I didn't. Do now.'

'Why did he want you to come here?'

'To tell you he's running late. But you're early. And you're supposed to be at the crossing point.'

'The what?'

'How did you two get in here?'

'Through the window. It was open, the door wasn't. Why is Aldous U going to be late?'

'He's busy.'

'Oh, busy, that's nice. I needn't have bothered then.'

'He's putting in an offer for a Withern Rise.'

'There's a Withern Rise for sale?' Her heart skipped a beat. 'Who's selling?'

'An Alex and an Ivan, that's all I know.'

'My parents…' she said softly.

'Your parents? You don't think they'd have told you if they were putting the house on the market?'

'They couldn't. Can't. I don't live there any more.'

This surprised him. 'You've left home?'

'You could say that.'

'Why, what happened?'

Before she could answer there was a muffled cry from Ric, who bounded back into the room, cast about him, and darted to the table, from which he snatched a large glass paperweight. He returned to the door – this time positioning himself behind it – seconds before the angular form of Gus O'Brien appeared on the threshold. In his left hand he held the rusty sickle Alaric had trodden on down by the river during his first visit.

'Well, well,' he said to Naia. 'You here too. All three of you together. How cosy. Where's the old boy?'

She stood up. 'He's about. Back any time.'

'Right. Well then…'

He came in, began sauntering round the room, swinging the sickle right and left. Books toppled, furniture cracked, ornaments went spinning and crashing.

'Stop that!' Naia shouted.

He did stop, and went to her, stood before her, eyes unreadable within the matted frame of colourless hair, the blade tapping rhythmically against his leg. Determined not to show fear, Naia stood stock-still, even when he raised the sickle slowly to his shoulder: that point could take her eye out with a single peck. They remained like this for some moments, until Gus, without a blink of warning, brought the blade down on the typewriter beside her on the table. Dull ring of metal on metal.

'Not his typewriter!'

'Oh, dear,' Gus said. 'Precious, is it?'

He placed a hand behind the machine and shoved. It resisted, but when he applied more effort it slid over the edge and crashed to the floor. In the appalled silence that followed, Naia glared loathing at Gus, to which he responded with a grin before his eyes drifted to the evidence of cottage industry on the table.

'What's this?' He picked up the recently-made pouch.

'Whatever it is, it's not yours,' she said.

His grin widened. He raised the pouch before her eyes, squeezed it provocatively, then inserted it, with a suggestive wiggle, deep into a hip pocket of his jeans. He then swung round to face Alaric, who'd not moved from the arm of the chair by the fireplace.

'And don't *we* look smart then?' Gus said. 'Which of 'em was it gave you the makeover? The tart or the old fart? I'm guessing him, shirt-lifter.'

'What?' Alaric said.

'Never failed to spot one yet. And when I do...'

As Gus advanced, slowly, swaggering for effect, Alaric stood up. 'I think you're mixing me up with someone else,' he said, eyeing the sickle nervously.

'You're the one that's mixed up,' Gus said. 'But don't worry. Relax. Uncky Gus gonna sort it for you.'

Alaric automatically took a step backward. His heel touched the rack of fire tools in the hearth. He looked down. The handle of an iron poker was within reach. Gus read his mind, gave a peculiarly light laugh, almost a giggle.

'Oh, yes, come on! Let's make a fight of it. That'll be fun.'

A small movement by the door caused Alaric to glance in that direction – a glance misinterpreted by Gus.

'Or maybe you want to leave us. Go on then, Nancy. Go for it.'

Behind him, unseen by him, Ric covered the space

204

between the door and Gus in three swift strides. The paperweight fell. The sickle clattered from Gus's hand as he dropped first to his knees, eyes fluttering in surprise rather than pain, then over onto his side, where they closed. Once down he remained perfectly still, one skinny leg twisted over the other.

'This is becoming a habit,' Ric said. 'One I could get to enjoy.'

'Took your time, didn't you?' Alaric said.

'At least I didn't just stand there. How feeble can you get?'

Naia dropped to her knees beside Gus and felt for a pulse. Relieved to find one, she stood up. 'What is his *problem*?'

'He's a psycho, that's his problem,' Ric said.

'Well, he won't be unconscious forever.'

'That could change. Give me a minute.'

'That would make you no better than him.'

'Oh, *please*!'

He went outside; stood on the path breathing shallowly. It had taken all his nerve to attack Gus a second time: the worry that it would go wrong; that he'd be the one to get hammered again.

Alaric and Naia, too, moved away from Gus. Even unconscious, utterly defenceless and vulnerable, there was something rather frightening about him.

'I saw him outside the other day,' Alaric said.

'Outside where?'

'Here. First time I came here. Who is he?'

'All I know is what I've seen,' Naia said. 'And I've seen far too much of him. Ric knows him.'

'Ric!' he sneered. 'What is it with this place? Something in the air that makes people shorten their names?'

'You never know. The air's none too sweet.'

'What do we do with him?'

'Who?'

'The psycho.'

'Don't know. Wonder if there's any rope about?'

'Why? You want to hang him?'

'Tie him up. He's dangerous. Did Aldous U say how long he'd be?'

'No, just to wait till he arrives.'

'How did you get here?' Naia asked.

'Same way you did, through the woods.'

'To this reality.'

He took the grey pouch from his pocket.

'Magic.'

She in turn produced the blue one that had brought her here.

'Any idea what these numbers mean?' she asked.

'Yours is the number of this reality,' he told her.

'Mine's the number of another, but it brought me here anyway because of what's inside.'

'But there's nothing inside. Just leaves and stuff.'

'That's all it takes.'

'But how can—'

A yell from outside cut her short. She whirled round. So did he. Gus was gone.

Alaric put the grey pouch in the wallet on his belt, but Naia was still holding hers as she rushed to the door. Ric lay on the path, on his back, arms folded over his head while Gus, sitting on his chest, beat him furiously with his fists. Naia dropped the pouch and threw herself onto Gus's back, an arm around his gullet. He reared up, jerked an elbow into her ribs, shook her off. She grunted as she fell on the path, but was up again at once, snatching a spade that stood in the earth nearby. She swung the flat of the blade at his head. Still vigorously pummelling Ric, Gus moved a second before it struck and the blade caught his shoulder instead, but it was a powerful enough swipe to topple him into a bank of what passed for flowers in the last days of this reality. Discarding the spade, Naia reached to help Ric up; a foolish gesture with Gus already clawing his way out of the flowers, the light of vengeance in his eye. He wasn't quite on his feet when Alaric, watching from the doorway, at last summoned the wit to act. He leapt forward, but, not driven by the other's passionate need to maim, was knocked aside with little effort. On his feet again, Gus's feral rage turned on the one who had intervened on his victim's behalf, as he'd turned on Ric when he came to her aid two days earlier.

'Right – whore! First I mash that fine face of yours to shit, then I *enjoy* myself!'

Knowing that she stood no chance against him, Naia ran to the open gate and into the forest. Gus went after her. Gaining their feet, Ric and Alaric made fleeting eye-contact – it wasn't easy looking at your non-reflected self – and by tacit agreement plunged after them. They were already lost to sight, but identifying their general direction wasn't a problem thanks to the oaths and murderous threats bellowed by Gus.

This double pursuit continued until silence fell as efficiently as the blade of a guillotine. It was a short silence, broken by a fresh shout of rage – 'Where did you go, *bitch*?' – but one which resumed when they burst out of the undergrowth an instant before Gus took a step forward and vanished. Ric could only gape, such departures being new to him, but even Alaric was startled when, almost immediately, a very different figure appeared in the space vacated by Gus O'Brien.

'You've met, I see,' Aldous U said, looking from one face to the other.

'And you just missed them,' said Alaric, while Ric remained speechless.

'Missed who?'

'Naia and the yob who peed on your garden.'

'Explain.'

'He was chasing her. I guess they both went to her reality. Not good news for her. He wasn't in a great mood.'

'It's unlikely that he'll have followed her,' AU said. 'The threads of his clothing should have taken him to his original reality.'

'Oh, I bet they'll be glad to see him. Did you buy the house?'

'I've put my offer in. They'll have to discuss it. Lap of the gods, if there were any.'

He pitched himself into the bushes. Unsure what else to do, they went after him, Alaric in the lead. AU seemed to take their following for granted.

'How did you two find one another?' he asked over his shoulder.

'He was at your house,' Alaric said. 'With Naia.'

'With Naia?'

'She arrived early, went straight there.'

'Oh, why doesn't that girl do as I *ask*?' AU cried with exasperation. 'It's not difficult. Three o'clock, there, wait. I don't know of a simpler way to put it. So they were chatting outside, were they?'

'No, chatting inside.'

Aldous U stopped and turned so suddenly that Alaric crashed into him. 'How did you get into my house?' he demanded of Ric, who had only just managed not to turn the halt into a farce.

'The window was open.'

'And you saw that as an invitation, did you?'

'I didn't do any harm. I didn't pinch anything. Well, a bit of food, but I was hungry.'

'How did Naia get in?'

'Also the window,' Alaric said.

'Well, obviously,' said AU, 'the door need never have been invented.'

They went on their way.

When they broke out of the forest and started up the path, AU made it plain that he wasn't happy that they'd left his front door wide open. He paused when he saw the pouch Naia had discarded in order to join battle with Gus. He picked it up. 'Why-oh-why are these so hard to hang *on* to?' He went inside. Ric and Alaric waited on the path. He was out again in no time: livid. 'Didn't do any *harm*?' he roared at Ric.

'That wasn't me, it was Gus.'

'Gus? Who's Gus?'

'The piss-artist,' said Alaric.

'There seems to have been quite a gathering here in my absence.'

He went back inside. This time they followed him. He was standing in the middle of the room, glumly surveying the wreckage.

'My poor old Underwood. Eighty, ninety years old, and some brainless oik tries to destroy it on a whim.' He noticed the sickle on the floor – 'I was wondering what happened to that' – then something else: 'There was a pouch on the table. I'd just filled it but had to leave before I could number it and put it away. Where is it?'

'The piss-artist put it in his pocket,' Alaric informed him.

'He didn't still have it when he followed Naia, did he?'

'Far as I know he did.'

'Then he'll have gone to the pouch's reality, not his own.'

'Well, at least he's out of our hair.'

AU sank dismally onto one of the chairs by the table. 'And potentially in a lot of other people's.' He stared at the floor. 'This is not good.'

'Do you know where I'm from?' Ric blurted suddenly.

'Don't you?' Alaric asked him.

'All I know is it's not here.'

Alaric turned to Aldous U. 'Do you?'

AU looked up. 'Do I what?'

'Know where he's from?'

'Why should I? Lot of realities out there.'

'You didn't have much trouble working out where I was from.'

'You weren't part of a gang that repaid my generosity by trashing my garden, stealing my chickens and murdering my cat.'

'I didn't do any of that,' Ric said.

'You were with them. You'll get no help from me, boy.'

'So you'll let him die here,' Alaric said.

Ric's eyes widened in alarm. 'Die here?'

'According to him, this reality's had it. All be gone soon. Nothing will survive. Except him. He's getting out. He'll be all right.'

AU scowled at Alaric. 'He didn't need to know that.'

'But now he does, so you've got to help him.'

'There's no "got to" about it. Even if I wanted to I wouldn't. I'd be interfering with the workings of a reality – something I'm careful to avoid these days.'

'Not that careful. The creep who went after Naia wouldn't have ended up where he has if you hadn't brought stuff back from there. If he does anything bad there it's down to you.'

'You think I don't *know* that?' AU barked. 'You think I'm not fully *aware* of that? The damage I've caused in my time!'

'Damage?'

'By being anywhere but here or my birth reality – merely *being* there – I make a difference that could lead to countless other differences, not all of them beneficial, some downright evil. Lives could ultimately be lost as a result of my simply saying hello to a stranger in a reality to which I don't belong.'

'Just by saying hello?'

'Even by being in the *vicinity* of that stranger if he notices me. If you haven't the wit to realise that, just take it as read.'

'You're talking about being somewhere you don't belong,' Alaric said. 'If you helped him get home – ' he found it impossible to refer to Ric either by that name or the full version ' – you'd be putting things right there, setting things straight. That'd be good, wouldn't it?'

'Whatever's happened in his reality has nothing to do with me,' AU said firmly. 'I'll not interfere, I tell you.'

'You interfere when it suits you. Those notes to Naia. Bringing her here. What's that if not interfering with her life?'

'Naia's a special case.'

'And me? Am I a special case too? I don't think so. All the stuff you've told me. Mind-blowing stuff that must change the way I think about the world, what I do with my...'

He stopped. Aldous U waited. He'd hoped this wouldn't happen. That a certain conclusion would not be drawn.

'Unless,' Alaric said slowly, 'you know something you haven't told me.'

'About what?'

'About my reality.'

AU looked him in the eye for a long silent time. Time enough to provide all the answer Alaric needed. The answer he least wanted.

'I'd like to be alone now,' Aldous U said then.

Alaric jolted out of his mournful reverie. 'Oh, I bet you would. So you can put us out of your mind, move to your "proper" Withern Rise, forget we ever existed.'

'Close the door on your way out, would you?'

Alaric tore the wallet from his belt and slapped it on the table. 'Returned!' he said, and stormed out.

Ric also headed for the door, but not with anger. Just before stepping outside he glanced back at the man who might have helped him get home, but had instead condemned him to death.

Aldous U looked away.

20: 43

Alone and very frightened in a world he now knew to be doomed, Ric wandered in the forest hoping to come across the others. With Gus out of the picture he had no qualms about calling to them, and this he did repeatedly; but the only reply was the odd flap of wings, or a frantic scuffle from some small creature he'd disturbed.

After a time he came to a particular tree that leant out over the water from the riverbank. This tree, with its coarse cocoa-coloured bark, bore a yellow-skinned fruit the shape and size of a ripe aubergine, at the heart of which lay a pellet of firm pink flesh that tasted not quite of apple, not quite of pear, but an approximation of both. Fruit had been the great sustainer for all of them, and it was Scarry who'd introduced him to this one, having previously sampled it and remained on his feet. Scarry liked first dibs at anything new. Maybe it was bravado, maybe his way of consolidating his position, but whenever they found an unfamiliar fruit he insisted on trying it before anyone else. Some varieties, which might not have been fruit at all, were so spiky, dubiously-coloured or unpleasantly sticky that even Scarry hadn't touched them, but he'd tried most of the more innocuous-seeming ones, almost all of which had turned out to be either very bland or rather bitter, though not inedible. Only once had they found a fruit that looked worth trying but had proved to be very much worth avoiding. It looked like a greengage and Scarry had rapidly consumed two, pulling a face at their tartness while trying to kid everyone that they were tasty in a good way. But just as the others were about to sample one each for themselves he had gone deathly pale, clutched his stomach, and spent the next five minutes heaving into the bushes.

Plucking one of the yellow aubergine-like fruits, Ric wondered where Scarry was – where any of them were – and why they were so quiet. He cracked the thick skin, eased it apart with his thumbs, and was about to bite into the fleshy nucleus when he glimpsed something between the reeds along the bank. He parted them with one hand and saw Scarry, sprawling just below the surface of the water, face up, staring at the dull yellow sky. The fruit fell from his hand. He staggered. His foot slipped. He sat down with a bump, and, very near the edge of the bank, clutched wildly for something to hold onto. His hand closed on what he took for a tree root, though it seemed rather less rigid than that. Only when he felt secure did he look to see what it actually was. It was a human ankle, sticking out of the grass. He leapt up as though yanked by the hair. Stared down at Jonno's twisted corpse. From there, he went on to discover, amid the withered grass and ailing weeds, two further reasons for the lack of response to his calls.

FLASH 4

It was rare these days for Naia to reflect that the village she drove through was not the one she'd known as a child. Somewhere along the way, over the years, its provenance had ceased to be relevant. Never very picturesque, central Eynesford was little more than a two-way street between narrow, nondescript eighteenth and nineteenth century houses, a few of which had been remodelled to accommodate small shops and businesses. The twelfth century Norman church was much as it had always been, but the old primary school across the road from it had been a private house for years. A little way past the church, where the housing estates began, a slightly raised platform of grass – littered with wrappers and drink cans from the Chinese chippy, bottles from The Cock and Bull – was a poor relic of a village green which would have been the communal hub for many a bygone generation. One of the cars parked haphazardly on the grass had skewed the sign that insisted that it was still The Green, whatever the year. This part of the village seemed coarser and uglier to Naia each time she returned. How different it must have been here in her grandfather's day. And Bishop Aldous, exchanging the nineteenth century for the twentieth, wouldn't even have recognised it in the twenty-first.

At The Green she turned right, onto a stretch of pitted tarmac that twitched between a plot of 1950s bungalows and a row of terraced houses (one of which bore a cement plaque dated 1899) before swinging left and becoming Withybank Lane. Two or three hundred metres further on she came to the ever-open five-bar gate of Withern Rise. She experienced a glow of pleasure on turning into the drive – the crunch of gravel beneath her wheels, the tunnel of reaching trees fanned by her headlights – and then she was drawing up in front of the house. The light had been left on in the porch to welcome her. She switched the engine off, released the seat belt, and was barely out of the car when Kate flung the front door back and rushed forward, arms outstretched – 'My darling!' – and then they were embracing as though they would never let go.

'Hugs aren't so easy these days,' Kate said, pulling back to eye the mound between them.

'A lot of things aren't so easy now.'

Kate went round to the back of the car and hauled the suitcase out of the boot. 'Is this it? Your entire wardrobe?'

'I've bribed my friend Michael to bring the rest down in his van next week.'

'Friend?' Kate said with interest.

'Just that.'

They went inside, where she helped Naia out of her coat. 'You two must be hungry.'

'All we want right now is to put our feet up and wallow in being stationary.'

'Drink, then.'

'Sworn off it till I'm free of the alien presence.'

'Even tea?'

'In a minute. Where's Aldous?'

'Upstairs, tarting himself up. He likes to look his best when you come. Don't let on that I told you.'

They went into the Long Room. Sat down on the couch. Naia sighed noisily. 'I can't tell you how good it is to be home!'

'Good to have you.'

'Don't give me that, my ears have been burning.'

'What do you mean?'

'You must have pictured it.'

'Pictured what?'

'That as well as me, very soon there'll be a squalling brat keeping you awake night after night, and soon after that he'll be scampering all over the place, breaking things, going where he shouldn't, ruining the viewing, conversations, everything. No more peace and quiet.'

'Peace and quiet's overrated,' Kate said.

'You say that now, but it's your home, you're used to not tripping over a disruptive supporting cast at every turn.'

'It's only my home because certain people allow it.'

Naia growled irritably. 'You know there's never been any question of "allowing it". Without you the place would've gone to seed after Dad died. Would have gone to seed before he died, if you hadn't been here.'

'Oh, I don't know.'

'I do. So no more talk like that please, unless you want a slap.'

She leant back, into the soft cushions of the big couch, the soothing atmosphere of the old house.

'I ought to tell you,' Kate said, 'that we'll have visitors at the weekend.'

'Visitors? Who?'

'Who do you think?'

'Not...?'

'Who else would I invite to commemorate your homecoming?'

'But that's brilliant! That's perfect!'

'Actually it was his idea. He was over the moon when he heard you were moving back. Said it's where you belong.'

'You said visit-ors...'

'Well, Chris is coming too, of course.'

'Oh. Yes. Of course.'

'I thought you liked Chris.'

'I love Chris,' Naia said. 'I really do. But sometimes...'

'I know. Just like to be alone. In-depth chats and all.'

'Yeah. Our stuff.'

'Already plotted for. I want to reorganise the shop and Chris has a fantastic eye for such things. I wouldn't be surprised if we weren't there all weekend. Fair bit of chinwag time for you two.'

'And some for me, I hope,' a voice said from the doorway.

Naia laughed with delight. 'Hello, my boy!'

A physical eighty-six, Aldous Underwood had the look of a rather preoccupied youth trying, not very

223

successfully, to play the part of an old man. He was very neat tonight, in a dark blue shirt and lightweight linen trousers. His hair, as thick as ever, with just a touch of grey, was carefully combed. Naia hauled herself to her feet and Aldous's cheeks warmed as she gathered him to her as well as she was able. Since their first meeting when she was sixteen, the boy inside the aging body had become a young man, though one with far less experience of the world than she, just five years his senior.

'What are you up to these days?' she asked when he was seated in the armchair facing her on the couch.

'Oh, you know. The usual. Not a lot.'

'Still corresponding with Rod?'

'Course.'

'And Lynne, now,' Kate said.

'Lynne?'

'Rod's half-sister. Our lad's a bit sweet on her.'

'I'm not!' Aldous said, but again coloured a little.

'She sent him a photo. Nice-looking girl. About his age too.'

He stared at his hands: thin, fine-skinned, undeniably elderly.

'Not this age,' he murmured.

This was one of his great sadnesses. No spirited lovers for Aldous Underwood. No physical love at all.

No choice but to be a solitary being, these two his only truly close friends and confidantes in all the world. He could not court women, even meet young men on equal terms, and the idea of spending time with people of his body's age revolted him. The truth about his life could never be told, or even hinted at beyond these walls. The press would have a field day. He would hate that.

'Well, I'm here now,' Naia said. 'Permanent fixture. And the three of us are going to have lots of talks and walks (whether you like it or not) and when he's old enough' – she pointed to the bump – 'we'll have picnics, go boating on the river, do all sorts of soppy family things together. But for the moment...Aldous?'

'Hullo?'

'I've had a long day, sod of a drive, and I have a craving for one of those toasted-cheese sandwiches of yours. How's about it, young feller me lad?'

He was up at once, all smiles – 'Right away, madam!' – and marching to the door: a man with a mission.

Part Four

THE EVITABLE CONCLUSION

1: 43/82

Aldous U had had a fitful night. Those damned Alarics, coming into his home and making him feel bad for minding his business in preference to theirs. Now that they'd pricked his conscience he felt – dammit, as if he hadn't enough on his plate! – an obligation to do what he could, for the one from the gang anyway. He was pretty sure where he belonged and could easily send him home, but if he helped him, what about his pals? He had no idea where they were from. Chances were, none of them had lived at a Withern Rise. They'd probably snuck into the grounds of their reality's version for a dare or something, hidden or strayed near the current crossing point, and been unfortunate enough to take the step that had brought them to R43, where they'd failed to realise that the way back was no more complicated than a step in the opposite direction. They might have ended up in any reality, of course. Other youngsters, taking that same unwitting step, could be just as lost in very different realities. Kids went missing all the time. They weren't all butchered, lured by paedophiles, sold into slavery. And they could disappear anywhere. Crossing points weren't exclusive to the Underwood See.

He'd woken in the early morning after less than three hours' sleep, knowing that he must at least attempt to locate the boys' home realities. He wasn't too hopeful of success, but he set off after breakfast to glean what he could from a fairly arbitrary selection of realities he'd not visited for some time. He allowed himself ninety minutes at most in each, concentrating his search on the village and nearer parts of the town. It seemed unlikely that the younger boys, at least, had come from much further afield. Unable to question anyone closely without arousing suspicion ('I'm looking for boys' – 'Hey, call the cops!') the best he could hope for was to overhear, in a shop or the street, or maybe the library, some mention of a lad who'd gone missing in recent months. He realised that by adopting such a casual method he might miss the very details he hoped to discover, but it was all he could do in the time available.

The day had not been a success. He'd failed to turn up any information whatsoever about missing boys. Late-afternoon now and he'd eaten nothing since breakfast but a small chocolate bar around eleven, drunk nothing but bottled water from a leather satchel whose main function was to shield the contents of the pouches he'd brought along. He crossed the market square to the Baker's Oven of the sixth reality of the day. Just a little snack, then off again. One more today and call it quits; start again in the morning with a fresh selection of pouches. Repeat the process the following day too, if necessary, but after that he would have to think of himself. Move the rest of his things out of R43 before it was too late.

There were still a couple of untried pouches in the satchel, but as he entered the café he decided that when he stole back into the garden of this reality's Withern Rise he would not use a pouch at all. Even without one, the step past the willow could take him to a reality he knew – impossible to predict where he'd end up that way – but there was always a possibility that he would find himself in a reality from which one or more of the boys had come. Occasionally, just occasionally, chance worked in your favour.

Naia was buying chocolate éclairs at the counter of the Baker's Oven when she saw the man she knew beyond any shadow of a doubt to be Aldous U. He was sitting in the poorly-lit café section at the back, frowning over something he was writing. She turned away so if he looked up he'd think she hadn't seen him, and, suddenly nervous, fumbled her change and flew outside with the bag of éclairs. She crossed the road at the lights and entered the market square car park, around which were a number of ornate iron benches. She seated herself on one of the benches to watch the shop, hardly daring to blink for fear of missing him. When he finally appeared in the doorway she raised the bag to her face, unlikely as it was that he would notice her from there, with a busy road, a car park, and pavements full of shoppers between them.

'Some funny people about,' said a voice.

Naia peeked round the bag: Lauren Hayle from her class, with some pasty-faced youth. They exchanged a laugh – no explanation needed for hiding behind a paper bag – and Lauren went on her way. As they went, she thought she heard the boy, who hadn't seen anything to laugh about, whisper, 'In't that that loony Underwood chick?' When she returned her gaze to the Baker's Oven, there was no sign of the man she'd intended to follow.

She jumped up, rushed to the pavement, waited impatiently for a break in the traffic, and hurried to the other side. There, she looked up and down the street, leaning, standing on tiptoe, hoping to catch a glimpse of the tall red-haired figure. In vain. Disappointed, she headed along the High Street. Recrossing the road at the lights by Flyaway Holidays, she cut through the cobbled lane between an estate agent's and a craft shop to Parable Road, on the far side of which lay the old woodyard bridge into Eynesford village.

In the village, about two thirds of the way along Main Street, she dipped into the paper bag and took out an éclair. She'd bought four, two for her, two for Kate (who she expected to throw histrionic hands in the air, then say 'Oh, what diet?', and bury her face in the first of hers). She was about to pass Mr and Mrs Paine's shop when she bit into the éclair. As her teeth closed, her toe caught a slight lift in the pavement. She tripped, ramming her nose into the chocolate icing. At the same instant someone came out of the shop. They collided. The man caught her arm, but the paper bag left her hand and opened out, scattering its contents. She looked up, a brown blob on the end of her nose, into the eyes of the man she'd failed to follow from the Baker's Oven.

Simultaneously recognising her, the man became shifty, stammered something incomprehensible, started away. Naia's imperious 'Wait!' brought him to a halt. She gathered up the street-soiled éclairs, dropped them in a wastebin, and, scrubbing her nose and sticky fingers with her hanky, walked him, like an apprehended felon, to the railings of the primary school on the corner. 'All these months,' she said, pinning him there, 'the mysterious letters, the instructions, the pouches, the missed meetings, and we bump into one another here, literally bump into each other! We could have met openly any time, any day, why all the…?'

He was staring at her, patently bemused. She lost it.

'Oh, cut it out! I know who you are! Why go on with it?'

But when his mystification merely intensified…

'You are Aldous U…?'

'Who?'

'You're not?'

'I-I'm just m-me.'

'But if you're not him…'

She considered the possibility that he wasn't who she'd believed him to be, accepted the twist with admirable aplomb, and started again, from a rather different standpoint. If he wasn't Aldous U, he was still the man she'd seen watching the house through binoculars, taking pictures of it. The man who'd run off when approached. So who was he? What had he been after? He wasn't going anywhere until he'd satisfied her on all counts.

He continued to stammer badly during the early part of the question and answer session that followed, but as he got used to it, and to her, the stammer receded. When he told her his reason for hanging round the house, she invited him back to meet Kate. He glanced about as if estimating his chances of making a break for it, but she took him by the arm and led him along the lane. He preceded her apprehensively through the side gate, but once on the path became calmer, as though resigned to what had to be done. By the time they reached the front step he seemed almost sanguine about the whole thing. Naia opened the door and called twice before Kate shouted 'On the phone!' from the Long Room.

She took him to the kitchen. 'What I don't understand,' she said, seating him across from her at the table, 'is why you didn't just ring the bell.'

'Oh, I couldn't, I—'

'But all that sneaking around! So...unnecessary.'

He started to stammer an apology, but she again cut him short; asked him to fill in the details. In his own time.

235

The last reality of the day, the 'chance' reality, turned out, as AU had hoped, to be one that he'd not visited previously. But there his luck ended. Venturing cautiously from the willow of a fairly average-looking north garden, he beheld a Withern Rise that lacked chimneys of any kind and whose walls were adorned with golden ivy rather than the more typical green-leafed variety. The second surprise was the man raking the driveway in front of the house, a gardener presumably, whose green skin did not stop at his fingers and thumbs.

In his time he'd come across a number of realities like this, where evolution had taken a different turn or two in its dealings with Homo sapiens, blessing them with a range of green and grey skin tones, and, in one that he'd happened upon, extremely large eyes. Since the early days, when he'd been pursued by a gang of teenage greys determined to lynch him for being differently coloured, he had never lingered openly in any of these realities. He'd ventured covertly into a few, however, usually at night, keen to learn what he could of their cultures and societies, and discovered that while alternative language structures had developed in some, others – locally at least – used a form of English that approximated to Elizabethan dialects. Such differences aside, the denizens of these realities worked for a living, lived in houses, drove cars, took their offspring to school, walked dogs, and worshipped hypothetical deities. During a couple of these clandestine explorations, AU overheard talk of winged alien craft spotted in the skies, encounters with brown and pink people, saw tabloid headlines shouting about visitors from outer space. This not only amused him greatly, but it put a whole new spin on UFOs and aliens in more familiar realities.

A youthful flirtation with the notion of extraterrestrial visitations had ended in his mid-teens when he acquired some understanding of the scale of the universe. When he realised the unspectacular size of the world on which he lived, and the position of its not-very-distinguished stellar system near the rim of a galaxy of around a hundred billion stars, it became unlikely in the extreme that we would attract the interest – or even notice – of people from other worlds. Add to that the fact that our galaxy is itself just one among billions and the idea became simply idiotic. The number of planets orbiting stars was so far beyond observable calculation that by any sane law of averages a great many must provide agreeable conditions for the development of intelligent species – not necessarily humanoid – at various stages of maturity. With such a plethora of worlds to take a peek at, and such colossal distances between them, why on earth, or anywhere else – and this was supposing such a feat were possible – would people from other planets even *think* of trekking all the way out here to see if there's anyone at home?

AU's discovery of green and grey realities cleared this up at a stroke, for him if no one else. Theories on the true nature of unusual flying objects had abounded for decades, falling under such headings as 'Imagination', 'Ignorance', 'Misinterpretation', 'Top-secret military applications', 'Ball lightning', and 'Electrically-charged plasmas of gas sculpted by air-flow into aerodynamic shapes'. Any or all of these were possible, but AU knew that there were no space-surfing discs (or whatever) from 'out there'. Most 'legitimate' UFO sightings were of craft from realities just a membrane away, where differently-adapted individuals used domestic aircraft unlike those developed in ours. And 'alien abductions'? It seemed reasonable to suppose that unscrupulous individuals from one or more green or grey realities had found crossing points into realities unlike theirs and carted off the odd gawping hayseed for interview or study – or maybe sideshow exhibition as 'a visitor from outer space'.

As he opened his gate in R43 at the end of this frustrating day, Aldous U heard the shiver of leaves nearby. He turned and saw Ric watching him. The boy had been waiting for him and did not dodge back, but said, rather plaintively: 'Please. Help me.'

'Help you what?' AU answered coldly.

'Don't leave me here,' Ric said. 'Not if it's all going to—'

He was cut short by an almighty roar that flipped his eyes and AU's skyward, where, as the sound expanded, mellowing into something akin to a long-suffering groan, they saw the heavens quiver, darken, and turn a swift purple, like a vast spreading bruise.

Aldous U shook himself, gave an anguished cry, and lurched up the path. Vaulting the wall, Ric bounded after him, demanding answers. He received none as AU fumbled with the padlock, threw the door back, and charged inside, where he dithered, attempting instant decisions he'd expected to have days to formulate. A celestial groan of even greater magnitude than the first activated him. He ran into the bedroom for the two framed photographs, which he put in a canvas bag as he returned to the main room, where he added papers, documents and keepsakes from various drawers and cupboards, all the while chastising himself for removing so few things while he had the chance. What distressed him most was the books he would now have to leave behind, many of them irreplaceable volumes from realities that no longer existed. He could have stashed far more than he had over the past few weeks in the little shed in the north garden of R36. Hastily selecting a handful of books from the stacks, allowing the rest to tumble, he shoved them in another bag, zipped it up, slid it across the floor to Ric – 'Take this!' – and set about levering up a number of floorboards. Beneath them lay a multitude of small pouches of various materials and colours. Darting about, picking and plucking from the array, muttering 'Which, which? Goddam memory! No *time*!', he crammed pouch after pouch into the satchel that had accompanied him to seven realities that day.

The satchel was no more than two-thirds full when the world fell silent, as though a switch had been flipped. He raced to the door, where Ric waited, trembling. High up in the sky, which had a dead look now, a confusion of long-tailed turquoise-and-crimson birds cawed and squawked as they converged on an orb of smeared darkness that had not been there before, whirling around it and each other with terror. 'Now where have *those* beauties been hiding?' AU said, before dashing back for one last item: the ledger in which he'd listed the thousands of realities he'd visited over the years.

With the book under his arm, the strap of the satchel on his shoulder, the canvas bag in his hand, he closed the door of the house: habit, though he left the padlock hanging. Ric was now waiting anxiously at the gate. Behind him, boughs groaned under their own weight; branches snapped; trunks crumbled.

'We'd best be off,' AU said. 'Rather quickly, I think.'

'We?'

'Unless you want to stay here.'

'I don't.'

'Where are your pals?'

'They're…lost.'

'Too bad. Missed their chance.'

Half-way along the path, AU stooped to touch a rectangle of flat grey stone, into which he'd scratched the name of his murdered cat. 'Farewell, old friend.' Rising, he continued on to the gate, but again stopped abruptly. 'My pipes!' He glanced back, tempted to return for them. The sound of a tree crashing down not so very far away caused wisdom to prevail. 'Well,' he said, 'never could play the damn things anyway,' and entered the forest, Ric hard on his heels.

The putrid flora was already a wasted tangle of brittle stalks and withering leaves. Trees creaked and splintered about them as they hurried past and through. The tight web of branches that had so reduced the overhead light pulled apart and came down in spinning clumps that had to be dodged.

Cats appeared, more cats than AU had known were there, beseeching him for assurance that everything would be all right. He could not meet their eyes.

By the time they reached the crossing point, the ground was as dry as ash, threatening to give way beneath them. AU fumbled with the clasp of the satchel, took out the first pouch he touched, and, gripping Ric by the arm, pulled him forward.

Within seconds of their going, Reality forty-three and all that it contained was no more.

4: 39

His name was Roderick Bishop. His mother had spent the first decade of her childhood at Withern Rise, and for the past twenty-one years had been running a motel and guest house with her second husband, Phil Gurney, in Dunedin, New Zealand. When Rod (her son from her earlier marriage to Maurice Bishop, a trombonist and tuba player from York) had announced that he was going to spend a few months in this part of England researching a book – he was an historian – she had prevailed upon him to go to Withern and take some photos for her. He had obliged, within days of landing at Heathrow in June, and at first his mother had been pleased merely to have the pictures, but then she developed further curiosity about the place it had become since she last saw it, and demanded written descriptions of it and its surroundings. The latest thing she'd asked him to do was go to the house and talk to the people who now owned it, find out how long they'd lived there, maybe get some pictures of the interior. Being of a nervous disposition, this latest request had given Rod sleepless nights, but three days ago he had finally managed to gear himself up to approaching the house and introducing himself. He'd not even made it to the end of the drive, however, when Naia spied him, whereupon he lost his bottle and once again made a run for it.

'Your mother lived here in the nineteen-forties then,' Naia said when she was up to date with all this. She'd heard it twice now, so it wasn't a question so much as a preamble to one.

'Yes.'

'You haven't told me her name.'

'Mrs Gurney.'

'Her first name. And her maiden name.'

'Her first name's Mimi. She was Mimi Underwood then.'

Naia beamed. She sprang from her seat. 'Don't move!'

He hardly dared to until she returned, breathless from a run upstairs, with an old photo album she placed on the table between them but did not open immediately. There was one more thing she wanted to know first.

'You dropped a pair of binoculars the other day.'

Reminded of his most recent flight from her, he again became agitated. 'Y-yes, I d-did, s-sorry, I—'

'It's all right, don't get in a state, I'm only asking.'

He took one of the deep, slow breaths that seemed to help his delivery. 'The binoculars are of no p-personal value.'

'Just as well. Someone else has them now. But I'm curious to know where you got them.' He told her. 'Oh,' she said. 'Ivan's shop.'

'Whose?'

'My...dad's.'

'Your dad's? Well that explains the name.'

'Name?'

'Underwood. Over the door. That's why I went in.'

'You could have asked him if he was a relative.'

'Oh, no. It was all I could do to buy something.'

'The binoculars.'

'Yes.'

'He never should have sold them. They belonged here. Still, they're back now. You know, I'm amazed your mum didn't know the family had returned to Withern. All these years and she had no idea.'

'Oh, she knew they'd *returned*,' Rod said.

'She knew? But…'

His mother, he explained, had told him about his Uncle Ray buying Withern back in the sixties, but her memories of their childhood home had not been as fond as Ray's and she'd never visited. In any case, any closeness that had existed between them as kids had faded during their teens, and once they left home for jobs in different parts of the country correspondence had never been better than sporadic. By the mid-seventies even birthday and Christmas cards had ceased to be exchanged, since when, over time, Mimi had come to assume that Rayner had either died or resold the property.

'Well, he *died*,' Naia said. 'But only five years ago. And as you see, he didn't sell up.' She was talking about the Rayner of her true reality, but this one's had died then too, same date, following the same illness, so the distinction was minimal.

'It was a similar story with Mum and Auntie Urse,' Rod said. 'That's her older sister.'

'Similar in what way?'

'The last we heard of Ursula was about twenty-five years ago. A postcard from Johannesburg, sent on her

245

behalf by a friend to inform Mum that she'd been thrown into jail for anti-apartheid activity. According to my dad – this was before the d-divorce – Mum washed her hands of Ursula then and there. She was always somewhere in the world stirring things up, Mum said. She doesn't approve of things like that. Pretty strait-laced about some things, my mum.'

Opening the photo album at last, Naia found a number of small black-and-white pictures of young Mimi in the garden at Withern Rise with her siblings and parents and a few others whose names were not recorded. Rod was transfixed. His mother had no such pictures, so this was a whole new world to him. A new old world. The only Underwood he'd known apart from his mother had been his grandmother, Marie, and she died when he was nine.

'Who's that?' he asked, tapping a finger on a picture of a young boy holding a home-made shield and a wooden sword, trying to look fierce.

'That's Aldous.'

'Oh, *that's* Aldous. I don't know much about him, only that he d-died in some nursing home up North, near my gran's.'

'Is that what your mum told you?'

'In some sort of coma for years and years, she said. Didn't think he could have lasted long after she left for New Zealand with Phil and me.'

'So she didn't know he'd died, just thought he must have, like Rayner? Does she think everyone's passed away if she hasn't seen them for a while?'

Rod smiled. 'I think she does tend to. Mum's not too sentimental about family. Or the past. "The past's another life," she always says. Or said. Sure changed her tune lately.'

'Aldous didn't die,' Naia said. 'He's still about all these years later. Lives here with us now.'

He was so astonished by this that, though he tried to respond, no words came.

'Nai?' Kate bellowed from the hall. 'Where are you?'

'Kitchen!'

Kate entered. 'I was talking to my old mate Tilly up in… Oh, didn't know you had…' She broke off; peered at Rod. 'Don't I know you?'

Naia said: 'Our personal stalker.'

Rod coloured slightly; began to stammer again. Naia reached over and put a hand on his arm. He fell silent. When Kate heard that he was the son of one of the great aunts Naia had never met, she was delighted.

'Well! You have a new cousin.'

She hadn't thought of that. 'So I do.'

'And I know someone else who might be interested to meet him.'

Naia smiled. 'So do I.'

They escorted Roderick Bishop to the great willow at the edge of the south garden, found Aldous nearby, fishing from the landing stage. From the side, the way he sat, the sun flecking the water behind him, he looked like a young boy. Round his neck he wore the brass binoculars his aunt had given him for his last birthday, when he was eleven.

5: 615/301/114

Slight as it was, the dizziness helped Ric overcome his surprise at finding himself under a healthy willow a mere step away from a disintegrating forest. 'Christ, I'm home.'

'No, you're not,' AU said, checking the number on the pouch. 'We have to go again.'

But Ric was already looking through the leaves in wonder. 'You think I don't know my own *garden*?' He laughed – his first real laugh for some time – and began to pass through.

'Stop, you fool!'

He didn't. AU went after him.

As they emerged from the tree an overweight man in his forties, charcoal-grey suit, red bow tie, metallic-blue laptop – 'What's all this?' – veered towards them from the path round the vegetable garden.

Ric froze. 'Who's he?'

'I'm guessing the owner.'

'The owner? But I've only been gone a—'

'This is not an Underwood reality. Next time listen to me.'

Too confused to argue, Ric allowed himself to be hauled back under the willow, where AU snatched another pouch at random. When he again gripped his arm, Ric protested.

'Will you stop that? We're not on a date.'

'If I didn't hold onto you,' AU said, 'you might end up where you want to be, but you'd be on your own. I haven't prepared you for that yet, so put up with it.'

He guided him past the trunk, into the reality from which the contents of the latest pouch had come. For Ric, apart from a further momentary disorientation, there was no noticeable change in their surroundings. AU assured him that whatever it appeared to be, it was not the same tree.

'Is it the one in my garden?'

'No. Again, no time to be selective.'

'But you do know where I'm from?'

'I believe so, but there's something I have to check before I can be certain. Wouldn't want to strand you in the wrong one, would we?'

'What do you have to check?'

'I need to know what your father does for a living.'

'He has a shop in the village,' Ric said, baffled.

'What sort of shop?'

'A crap shop.'

'What kind of crap?'

'Rubbishy old furniture and stuff.'

'In that case,' AU said, opening the satchel once more, 'it's just as well I made a point of grabbing that one.'

Ric went to the edge of the tree and peered out. No man in a suit this time, but about half-way between the willow and the hawthorn hedge there was a sand pit, in the centre of which stood a blue-and-red plastic castle, about four feet high. 'I had one like that when I was little,' he recalled.

'Whatever it is, it's not yours and you're a big boy now,' AU said. 'Here it is. Ready?'

Ric returned to the trunk. 'As I'll ever be.'

AU gripped his arm one last time and they stepped forward together. More alert to the process now, Ric noticed the almost imperceptible quiver that told him that something had happened even though the tree appeared unchanged.

'Are we in the right one now?'

AU flipped open the leather satchel and popped the pouch in. 'If we're not, there's more than one missing Alaric.' He took the bag Ric had been carrying for him since R43. He now had three bags about his person, as well as the large book under his arm. 'A supermarket trolley would have been handy,' he muttered.

'Is it all right for me to go out there?' Ric asked, nervous where he hadn't been the last two times.

'Well it *is*,' AU said, 'but you can't just walk in and expect your parents to throw their arms round you without asking questions.'

'Well, no. Bound to be questions.'

'Which means explanations. They last saw you in July. There were no clues as to where you'd gone; the police were called, there was a big search, your picture was in the papers, and in a few weeks you were just another missing person to everyone except your folks. But it's late October now, and right out of the blue you stroll across the garden, a bit thinner, looking like you've been sleeping in a ditch. "Hey Mum, hey Dad, what's for tea?" What do you think they're going to do? Lay an extra place and say "Have a nice time, son"?'

'I'll just tell them what happened,' Ric said.

'What, that you've spent the past three months lording it with the flies and a bunch of lads in the forest of another reality? Yeah, that'll cover it.'

'I could say I lost my memory.' Aldous U pulled a face. 'Well what else can I say?'

'I can't tell you that. I wouldn't know what to say myself in your position. I just wanted to make you aware of the difficulties ahead.'

'Consider me aware. I'll just have to get through it.'

'Fair enough.'

AU rummaged in the satchel for the pouch that would take him to the next reality. Ric shifted about uncomfortably, wanting to say something, finding it hard.

'What is it?' AU said, glancing up.

'I'm...you know.'

'No, I don't know. Spit it out.'

'I'm sorry about your house. What we did. And your cat.'

AU found the pouch. 'I thought you denied responsibility.'

'Yeah, but like you said, I was there. I could have stopped some of it.'

'Well, it's done. Over.' AU found the pouch he was looking for. 'Go on now. I won't wish you luck because it wouldn't help. Shoo.'

He waited while Ric pushed his way out of the willow. Then, putting the pouch in his pocket, he took the step to the reality that would be his home from now on, as it was in the beginning.

6: 39/47

When a reality of some maturity passes, there's often a ripple effect among those of its neighbours with which it has much in common. More notable phenomena generally include a flurry of movement – a kind of buffeting, as of strong winds in transit – around the edges of the earth's tectonic plates, and, here and there, unseasonable weather and temperatures. Coincidentally – or not – there's also, quite often, an increase in violent crime and terrorist activity, and the international suicide rate briefly soars. R43 was one of the rare realities that had no bank of twins, yet its extinction was so dramatic that shock-waves triggered a series of unnatural events in a number of others. Torrential rain fell for twelve-and-a-half minutes on the Sahara of Realities eighteen and sixty-four, an earthquake among the Aleutian islands of Reality one-one-nine caused a Pacific-wide tsunami that claimed the lives of a hundred and eighty-three people, sudden high winds in Reality ninety-seven whipped the roofs off eleven recently-renovated Outer Hebridean crofts, a vast tract of Tasmanian bush in Reality eight-seven-nine spontaneously combusted, and whirlwinds carried off three trucks in two versions of Kazakhstan, six cars on Autobahn 5 in Realities twenty-eight, twenty-nine and three-one-five, and a busful of nuns returning from a trip to the Lourdes of Reality six-seven-two.

Only in two realities, and a particular part of these two, was there a storm that raged for over an hour. In one of these, as the heavens howled, rain battered the garden, and lightning flashed across the French windows of the Long Room, Naia said: 'We can't leave him out there in this!'

'No, we can't,' Kate agreed, 'and he'll just have to lump it!'

'You're not going out there?' Ivan said as they ran from the room. They ignored him, snatched their coats from the rack and jumped into inappropriate shoes. Kate tucked Ivan's raincoat under her arm. As they opened the front door, the garden was again illuminated by a flash. They both jumped back.

'My foot!'

'Sorry!'

Then: outside, running through sheets of rain that

lashed Naia's hood and soaked Kate's hair, and a furious wind that did its damnedest to drive them back. Reaching Aldous's willow, they hurtled through its flailing green whips to where he sat bolt upright, cloaked in his sleeping bag, a terrified young boy crying for the mother he'd lost in his forty-third year while he slept. They pulled him to his feet and discarded the sleeping bag. Draping the raincoat about him, they rushed him, between them, into the wind and rain – and a shaft of light so brilliant and close that it brought a shriek from all three mouths.

Within a few steps, a deafening overhead boom brought Aldous to a petrified halt. While fighting his reluctance to proceed, Naia caught a flare of white at the edge of her eye, something small, racing, and remembered her cat; but there was no time for distractions. Bawling assurances, they bundled the cowering Aldous across the lawn and round the corner of the house to the front porch. Thrusting him into the hall, they cast the coat to the floor and drew him into the Long Room, where Ivan's 'Bloody hell!' was brushed aside, and he with it, to watch scowling from the wings while his unexpected house-guest was soothed and cosseted.

The storm was no less vivid or strident in Alaric's reality, but there was no one to rescue there. He and

Kate, sharing a heady combination of exhilaration and alarm (to Ivan's comfortable amusement), remained at the French windows of their Long Room.

'Wouldn't like to be out there now,' Kate said.

'Me neither.'

What no one was in a position to see from either version of the house was the sliver of white light that struck a gravestone below the wall that separated the garden from the old cemetery. The stone was not shattered, but its surface was blasted so effectively that henceforward it would be impossible for the untrained observer to guess how old it was, precisely who it commemorated, or when he or she had been lain to rest beneath it. There remained just one readable word on the stone: UNDERWOOD.

7: 39/47

Next morning, post storm, there was an uneasy feeling in the air. The sky wore its greys and blues awkwardly, as if they did not quite match its intentions. A jittery breeze caused leaves to fret. Birds perched silently. 'Feels like war's been declared,' both Kates observed – in one reality to Ivan and Naia, in the other to Ivan and Alaric – as they approached the south garden to inspect a limb wrenched off the Family Tree. It looked odd, sprawling across the lawn in its shroud of shrivelled leaves.

'Well, now that we know bits can fall off it in the slightest draught,' both Ivans said, 'it's got to come down, no question.'

In Naia's reality, Aldous kept to the Long Room – where he'd passed the night on the couch – until Ivan left for the shop. As he was going, Ivan, in the hall, said, rather too loudly: 'I'll be home for lunch, by which time I expect the house to be my own again.'

When he slammed the door after him, Naia, in the kitchen with Kate, said: 'Moody today.'

'Territory invaded,' Kate said.

'Well, we can't just chuck him out.'

'Which of them are we talking about?'

Aldous wandered in shortly afterwards.

'How was it?' Naia asked him. 'Spending a night under an actual roof. Not so bad, I bet.'

'I'd better go,' he said, admitting nothing.

'You'll have some breakfast first,' Kate said.

'No, I've still got some bread out there from yesterday.'

'Ah, but here you can have it hot and crisp, fresh out of the toaster.'

'And we've got a new plum jam,' Naia put in.

He gulped. 'Plum jam?'

'Home made,' said Kate. 'Or so it says on the label.'

Minutes later they were leaning against the sink watching him eat his toast with sly relish.

'Like a big kid,' Kate whispered.

'*Exactly* like a big kid.'

They chuckled conspiratorially.

Aldous polished off four rounds before informing them that the jam wasn't like Maman used to make and popping into the adjoining bathroom, converted from the old utility room for his sole use, with a door to and from the garden. 'Off now, then,' he said when he looked in on them again.

He started to retreat, but Naia said: 'Come out the front.'

'The front? No, this way'll do me.'

'You've been our guest. Today it's the front door, like anyone else who stays the night.'

As with the toast and jam he gave in with his rendition of an elderly huff of reluctance, and the three of them went out to the hall. But when they opened the front door, he did not leave immediately. Last night was the first time since his return that he'd entered any part of the house other than the kitchen and his personal bathroom. Rushed in from the storm so unceremoniously, he'd been in no state to take anything in, but he was calm now, and nothing like as rattled as he usually was within walls.

'So different,' he murmured.

'Different good or bad?' Naia asked.

'Just different.'

He left.

'We'll get him indoors yet,' Kate said, closing the door and heading upstairs.

'I know someone who won't be celebrating if we do,' Naia called after her.

When the bell rang a few minutes later, and kept on ringing, it was she who opened the door. Aldous stood on the step, drained of colour.

'What is it?'

He didn't answer. Seemed unable to. He tugged at her sleeve. She slipped her shoes on and followed him round the corner and along the side of the house. He kept hold of her sleeve, leading the way. She asked more questions as they went, but he answered none of them. What was it that had got him so worked up?

She found out as soon as they rounded the next corner, on the river side. In a little rockery that Kate had constructed a few days earlier, curled up in a tight white ball, was her cat.

'Alaric!'

She fell to her knees. Touched him. He was cold and stiff. She gathered him up tenderly. The white fur around his nose was tangled and dirty, suggesting that he'd tried to burrow into the earth. His eyes were half open, but there was no life in them. Naia looked up at her friend, bending over her.

'Oh, Aldous.'

He straightened up, stepped back, stumbled about as though unsure which way to go, then started running, in the same ungainly way she herself ran when agitated or in a hurry, not stopping until he reached his willow, into which he plunged, sobbing uncontrollably.

8: 47

About an hour after Aldous rang the doorbell in Naia's reality, the same bell rang in Alaric's. 'Yes?' Kate said to the stranger on the step.

'Good morning. I wonder if I might speak to Alaric?'

'Alaric? Ye-es. And you are…?'

But he'd turned away as if dismissing her. She half closed the door on him and hastened along the hall. Music in the distance, up above.

'Alaric!'

No answer. She ran upstairs and along the landing. Reaching the corner bedroom, she knocked. The music, much louder here, did not cease. She knocked harder.

'What!'

'Someone to see you!'

'What?'

'SOMEONE TO SEE YOU!'

The music stopped. The door opened.

'It's a man,' Kate said. 'At the front door, for you.'

'Who is he?'

'Didn't say. No one I know.'

He went ahead of her down the stairs, along the hall; pulled the front door back.

'Come with me,' Aldous U said at once.

'Why? Where?'

'Just come. Quick now.'

Alaric turned to Kate, a little way behind him, trying not to seem nosy.

'Got to go out.'

'There's nothing wrong, is there?'

'No,' he said uncertainly.

The step had been vacated while he spoke to Kate. He jammed his feet into his shoes, snatched his jacket, hurried after AU, who was already in the north garden. Catching a glance back at the southern sky, Alaric also looked, and saw, amid the blue-grey above the Family Tree, a quivering red sphere that was not a sun.

'That's weird.'

'Come on!'

When they were both within the willow, AU reached into the leather satchel slung over his shoulder; took out a small transparent phial with a plastic stopper in the end.

'What's that?'

'Urine sample-bottle. Sometimes called a Universal Pot. Pretty funny when you consider what I use it for.'

'Which is?'

'It's going to take us to the place its contents come from.'

'But there's nothing in it.'

'Precisely.'

'Is that supposed to make sense?'

'It doesn't have to.'

AU took him by the arm and, with a single step, walked him from that reality into—

9: –

—nothing at all.

Alaric's first reaction was to grab hold of something, but there was nothing to grab. AU first steadied him, then walked him away from their point of arrival. When they halted, Alaric stared helplessly about him at a perfect white space without blemish, contour or form. There was no ground, no sky, no horizon, no sense of distance or volume. It was impossible to tell whether it went on forever or ended an arm's reach away.

'What kind of…' Far too loud in this boundless space. 'What kind of reality's this?' Almost a whisper, but sufficient.

AU returned the empty sample-bottle to the satchel and took out a fawn-coloured pouch. Even the sound of his hand brushing the leather could be heard here.

'Did I say it was a reality?'

He popped the pouch into one of his jacket pockets and strolled several paces in one direction before turning sharply in another, as though needing to stretch his legs. His feet made no sound and did not sink, as they would have into snow or some other soft surface. Nor did he cast the slightest shadow, and when next he spoke he had no need to raise his voice in spite of the distance between them.

'Let me tell you about a dream I had when I was a lad.'

Alaric said nothing. He couldn't, any more than he could move. This utterly barren realm frightened him more than any place he'd ever seen or imagined.

'Same dream night after night, went on for almost

a week,' AU said, starting back towards him. 'It was of a featureless white room, no door, no windows, quite empty. Each night I'd go downstairs to try and shake it off, but when I went up again, went back to sleep, I'd be in that room once more.'

Alaric tried to focus. Any distraction.

'What happened?'

'Happened?'

'To you, in the dream?'

'Nothing happened. It was terrifying.'

'You think it was a trailer for this…whatever it is?'

'I'll leave you to speculate on that,' AU said, walking past him. 'Something to think about while I'm gone.'

Panic. 'You're leaving me here?'

'It's all right, don't worry, I won't abandon you.'

'I can't stay here by myself!' Too loud.

'You'll have to. Can't go where I'm going. Just stay away from the point at which I disappear, or we may never see you again.'

'But what do I do while you're away?'

Aldous U waved a hand around – 'Mingle' – and took the step that left Alaric alone in the midst of absolutely nothing.

The cat's death still filled their minds. Aldous's particularly. Burial somewhere in the garden had been agreed upon, but 'somewhere' was as far as they'd got. Kate was trying to distract him and Naia by marshalling their forces in a grand tidy-up. While the fallen bough was the most conspicuous casualty, a number of smaller plants had been uprooted, and scraps from many more scattered to the furthest reaches of the garden. While Kate helped Aldous round his side of the house, Naia, preferring to be alone, gathered loose material from the lawns at the front, dumping it in the old wheelbarrow on the drive.

'Some storm, by the look of it.'

She glanced up. Mr Knight.

'Didn't you see it?'

'I was away last night. The old oak hasn't come out of it too well.'

'No.' Pause. 'Alaric died.'

'Alaric?'

'The cat you gave me. He was out in it. Fright, we think.'

'Ah, poor little mite.'

'It's my fault. I should have made sure he was indoors.'

'Don't blame yourself,' Mr Knight said. 'Very independent spirit, that one. I doubt you could have coaxed him in.'

'We coaxed Aldous in.'

'Cats are more self-willed than humans.'

'But I should have tried.'

She continued stuffing debris into the wheelbarrow, mildly irritated when Mr Knight, though the conversation seemed to have ended, did not move away. She was about to ask him if he'd come to lend a hand when the path, the lawns, everything within and around her field of vision, very briefly but dramatically turned ice-blue.

'What was that!?'

'Naia,' Mr Knight said. 'Will you come with me please?'

'What was it?'

'Post-storm shadow. There's something in the north garden you have to see.'

'Post-storm shadow? I've never heard of such a thing.'

'Nevertheless. Come on. It's quite urgent.'

'Oh, not more damage.'

'You have to see for yourself.' He started away.

'Did you two see that?' Kate called from the corner of the house.

'Couldn't miss it,' Naia answered.

'Naia! Now!'

Startled by his tone – so unlike him – she said: 'Mr Knight wants to show me something.'

'More damage?' Kate asked.

'That's what I said.'

'Shall I come?'

'No.' This from Mr Knight, very firmly, still walking.

Naia removed the gardening gloves she'd borrowed from Kate, draped them over the side of the wheelbarrow, and set off after him. When she realised that he was heading for the willow, she became anxious. Had he found something intended for her eyes only? Another of those pouches perhaps? He reached the tree, waited for her, holding an armful of leaves aside for her.

'In here.'

As he said this he looked over her head. Turning, she saw a blood-red glow, like a bodged attempt at a sun in an uninspired watercolour sky.

'Another post-storm effect,' he said before she could ask, and rustled the leaves to indicate urgency.

Inside, though the light was low, she could see no evidence of further calamity. She was even more relieved that there was no pouch that would have to be explained away.

'What was it you wanted to show me?'

'Round the other side.'

He took her arm, began steering her round the trunk.

'Oh, I don't think we ought to go round h—'

She didn't finish. In any reality.

11: –

Alaric advanced, step by very tentative step, across the flawless white space. There was no sense of connection with any 'ground', yet he did not feel that he was floating. He paused once and stamped his foot. It descended with the anticipated force, stopped at the right level, but there was no impact, and no sound of any. Walking further, he looked back to determine how far he'd come. The soles of his shoes were far from spotless yet they'd left no marks, which suggested that nothing from outside was permitted to leave evidence of its passing here. It must be some sort of non-reality, with its own physical laws – which could amount to no laws at all. But he was breathing normally, so there must be air. Or was there? Could he be going through the motions of breathing merely out of habit? He held his breath. Counted sixty seconds, sixty more, another sixty – and felt no need to expel air, or draw any.

He continued to walk about for something to do, trying not to think that a written guarantee had not accompanied Aldous U's pledge to return. Suppose he didn't keep his word; never had any intention of keeping it. He'd be stuck here forever. Long as he lived anyway. *Could* he live here? Could he die here? If nothing changed here, maybe he'd remain his present age for all eternity. If that happened, what about the need to eat, drink, sleep? Would he have such needs? This had to be the loneliest place any imagination could conjure, yet just a step away universes pulsed and flared, life teemed, realities flourished in countless variations, bustling independently through all the horrors and absurdities that 'humanity' was capable of. But here, from here, it was as if none of that existed, as if night never fell, stars never appeared in any firmament, nothing grew, developed, evolved. What a place. To be forced to stay here, where time had no meaning outside of your head. You'd go barmy. Stark staring—

It happened in a split second.

One instant he was in that featureless abyss, the next he stood by the cemetery wall in the grounds of Withern Rise, gasping for breath he suddenly needed.

Struggling to adjust, he stared around. The little apple tree he should be standing near had been replaced by a wooden shed that smelt of creosote. Up above, a fine blue sky; far to the right a cylinder of smoke unravelling from a corner of the vegetable garden; to his left, just past a Family Tree that had not lost a limb to a storm, a grass tennis court; by the house, four unfamiliar adults watching children play some dashing and darting game – until they noticed him, when they all stopped what they were doing and stared across the garden, at him.

'Mr Ochs! Who's that?'

A man rose like a genie from a nearby bush.

'Oo're you?' Alaric's lack of response – he was stuck for any – was evidently suspicious, for the gardener said to his employer, 'Nothera them yobs, miss. Duworry, I'll see 'im orf,' and came round the bush wielding a garden fork.

Alaric took a step backward. The wall prevented further retreat. But not for long. Suddenly there was no wall, no garden, no one coming at him, and he was falling, falling silently, onto nothing. He remained there, sprawling, too stunned to even think of moving, until—

'Sunbathing?'

He lifted his head. A long way off, where the

willow in the north garden had been moments before, stood Aldous U. With Naia.

12: –

Naia gaped about her, seeking something to focus on, finding it only in Alaric, getting up from what looked like nothing and walking towards them, also on nothing. When he said 'Her too now?' it barely registered that his words were crystal clear even though he was some distance away and had not raised his voice. She turned to her companion.

'Mr Knight, where are we? What's going on?'

'Mr Knight?' Alaric said across the void. 'Why'd you call him that?'

'It's his name,' she told him.

'That's not his name. He's Aldous U.'

Anywhere else, another occasion, she might have laughed. 'Where did you get that from? He's Mr Knight, he helps in our garden. Tell him,' she said to the man who'd brought her here.

He confirmed this. 'I am John Knight.' But added: 'And Aldous U.'

She frowned. 'What are you saying? I know who you are. I've known you since April.'

'You've known me since January,' he said.

She shook her head. 'That was another Mr Knight, another…somewhere else.'

He shook his. 'There was only ever one.'

'What?'

'And I'm still working with your mother as well as with Kate. Bit of a stretch, two part-time gardening jobs. Never worked so hard in my life.'

'Am I missing something here?' said Alaric, closing the gap between them at a fair lick.

But this, for now, was a conversation he had no part in.

'You can't be both Mr Knights,' Naia said.

'I am, though.'

'Both Mr Knights and Aldous U? No.'

'Yes. Sorry.'

'But the letters. You handed me one of them – as Mr Knight.'

'Necessary, I'm afraid. There was no reason to suppose that you would look in the message hole in the foreseeable future, so I was forced to give it to you in person.'

She almost exploded at this. 'In person!'

'You don't have to shout here,' Alaric said.

'I'll shout if I want to,' she retorted, but more quietly. She closed her eyes. Intending to count a slow ten, she only managed five before opening them again. Glaring at Aldous U.

'Why me? Why *me*?

'Why you? Because, to my knowledge, there's just one other Naia who knows that hers is not the only reality, and—'

She gasped. 'Another Naia?'

'—and she still has both of her parents and the life she's always had, while you've lost everything yet have come through so bravely. I felt that you deserved to know more.'

'I want to know *everything*,' she said. 'The reason for all the play-acting, the secrecy, and—' she cast bleakly about her '—what this is.'

'I can tell you what this is,' Alaric said. 'It's Hell without the fire and brimstone. Or anything else.'

He might as well not have spoken.

'Let's take the gardening persona first,' Aldous U said to Naia. 'You saw the patch of ground around my house. It was quite a nice little garden once, but over the past twelve months or so the soil became unworkable. The reality was dying, you see. Towards the end of last year I began to long for a proper garden, but there was only one I really wanted.'

'Mine,' Naia said.

'Yours. As was. The one my dad once tended.

I offered my services to your mother, and might have been content with that to this day if you two hadn't met.'

'How did you know about that?'

'I knew about it as soon as it happened. I've developed a kind of sixth sense about inter-reality activity. The local variety anyway. Side-effect of having spent so much time in them, I suppose. Whenever I pick something up on the personal radar, and if it seems relevant to the Underwood See of my cluster, I investigate.'

'The Underwood See?' Naia said.

'Don't ask,' said Alaric. 'We'll be here forever.'

But it was he who enquired what AU meant by his 'cluster'. And AU answered him.

'A while ago I conducted a major overhaul of my files. I had pouches for so many realities that the numbers had got ridiculously high. I dumped those I doubted I'd want to return to, and re-numbered the rest, grouping them by various criteria or associations. The group that I call my cluster – Realities thirty-five to forty-eight – includes your two and R43, my former base-reality. No reality is closer than any other, of course, but by numbering them in that way it felt like having neighbours. True neighbouring realities.'

Naia said: 'Your *former* base-reality?'

'R43 ended late yesterday afternoon. I got out just in time.'

'What about the boys?' Alaric asked.

'I returned the other you to his home reality, as "requested".'

'And the rest?'

'It happened so quickly. They were nowhere to be found at the end.'

'So they died.'

'There was nothing I could do.'

'This isn't what's left of that reality, is it?' Naia said.

'Oh no, this is something else entirely.'

The timing of this reply, though not calculated, was perfect, for within a beat of its utterance the empty space in which they stood was transformed into the north garden of Withern Rise, under a perfect blue sky in which birds—

And then it was gone. All of it. The life, the colour, the world.

Naia reeled. 'What was *that*?'

'A new reality,' Aldous U said, unfazed. 'Fully charged and populated in a jiffy, extinct a jiffy later. That's the way of it for most of them. Realities come and go like the flashes of fireflies.'

Alaric might have mentioned the slightly longer-lived one he found himself in shortly before their arrival, but Naia, though thoroughly bemused, was already there with her next question.

'What was the point of those letters? You could have just given them to me. Or better still told me what you wanted me to know.'

'It was never my intention to deceive you,' Aldous U said with genuine humility. 'The first letter wasn't meant for your eyes at all. It was just one of the many flights of fancy I've committed to paper over time. I dropped it in the tree shortly after I began helping Alex in the garden – weeks before you found it.'

'Even if that's true,' she said grudgingly, 'it doesn't explain the letters in my present reality, in June and this week.'

'Your present reality?' Alaric said.

'Now they *were* for you,' AU said – to Naia. 'It was your transfer to that reality that made me approach Kate with an offer of garden help, as I had your mother three months earlier. I wanted to be about in case you couldn't handle it. As it turned out you could, so I kept quiet. Stayed around to keep an eye on you, but that's all. I only put the letter in the tree in June because something was happening that might have harmed you. I wanted to warn you to watch your step.'

'What something?'

'It doesn't matter now, it's past, didn't touch you after all. The point is, there was no need for further correspondence – until last weekend, when I decided to tell you everything. And I wanted you to see R43 before it vanished forever. It may not have been very pretty towards the end, but it was an unusual reality, you have to admit.'

'Tell me which is the real you,' Naia said coolly. 'Mr Knight or Aldous U.'

'I was christened John Aldous Knight,' he replied, 'though the middle name was at my father's insistence. Mum wasn't keen on it. You see, shortly before I was born my dad came across a family skeleton in some document found among his late father's papers which showed that in her twenty-second year his grandmother, Dorothea, while married to a rather dour Presbyterian pharmacist named Holden Knight, had a child by the local Bishop.'

'Not Bishop Aldous.'

'The one and only.'

'And that's why you call yourself Underwood? Because of that connection?'

'I don't call myself Underwood.'

'Of course you do. What else could the "U" stand for?'

'Well, it could stand for...let me see. Unsworth? Uttley? Utteridge? Unger? How about Uxley?' He laughed. 'Aldous Uxley – I like that!'

Naia was less amused. 'If your name isn't Underwood, what is it?'

'Uxenden,' said Aldous U.

'Uxenden?'

'My mother's maiden name.'

'Really?'

'Really.'

'And all this time...'

'The people who bought Withern Rise from your family in the late nineteen-forties didn't require my dad's services, so he was out on his ear. He got menial work here and there, but less and less as time went on – gardening was all he knew – and he grew bitter about his increasingly lowly status. Descended from a wealthy churchman, and here he was clearing out drains and sweeping the streets to feed his wife and kid. This resentment led him to develop an ambition to see me elevated to the social level of his grandfather's legitimate heirs. He wanted me to study hard and achieve the kind of qualifications that would lead to a well-paid, suit-wearing position and my becoming a respected man in the community. But it wasn't for me. I didn't aspire to such things. All I wanted was to travel, see the world.' He laughed again. 'If I'd only known the *worlds* I would see!'

'This is fascinating,' said Alaric, unfascinated. 'But how about telling us why you brought us here?'

'Because of our very different ambitions for me,' AU went on as though he hadn't spoken, 'Dad and I ceased to get on. Things went from bad to worse until he no longer even looked at me. I remember one winter evening when I was sixteen. The two of us sat in the living room of our cottage in School Lane. I was trying to explain how I felt about things, smooth things over between us, and he was reading the paper as if I wasn't there.'

'I know how *that* feels,' Alaric muttered.

'Suddenly he got up, walked across the room, turned the light out, and closed the door behind him, leaving me in darkness. Then, the morning of my seventeenth birthday, instead of a card he left a note for me to see after he went to work. In it he said that he hoped I wouldn't be there when he got home. I took the hint – and a room above the ironmonger's in Stone and, in retaliation, made it known that I would no longer bear my father's name but be known as Aldous Uxenden.'

'Uxenden or not,' Naia said, still smarting over the months of deception, 'you must have known I'd take you for an Underwood when you signed those letters Aldous U.'

He looked contrite. 'As I said, I didn't think you'd see that first letter.'

'You meant me to see the others.'

'A precedent had been established.'

'And you put "Withern Rise" at the bottom.'

'Withern Rise was the name of my house in R43.'

'Yes, but still...' She floundered.

'When I was very young I wrote cryptic notes, often in lemon juice, which I signed John Aldous K above my address, printing "To the Finder" on envelopes I made with waterproof paper from the mill where my mum worked. I closed the envelopes with a wax seal that bore the letter "A" – the same stamp I use today, given to me by my father when I was eight or nine to remind me of my illustrious namesake and forebear. I would post the envelopes in this hidey-hole or that, ostensibly to be found by a stranger or relative, though more often than not the finder was me. I would come upon them with feigned surprise and warm the pages over a candle to reveal the message. Last January, I put that first letter in the tree to commemorate my return to the garden I knew in early childhood, when I would toddle round after my dad while he was working. No longer needing to discover it myself, however, it remained there till you found it.'

'Pity you didn't use lemon juice that time,' Naia said. 'It wouldn't have occurred to me that those sheets were anything but blank.'

'I still don't get the reason for the two names,' said Alaric.

'In most realities I'm Aldous Uxenden,' AU replied, looking directly at him for a change. 'But in a few, where I have dealings with Withern Rise residents who might wonder about the bloodline of someone called Aldous, I stick to John Knight. It's simpler that way.'

'Simpler,' Naia said. 'Rich, coming from you.'

'So what do we call you?' Alaric asked.

He waved a hand around. 'Here, I'm not fussy.'

'I'd like to know why you didn't show yourself the day you ran me out of the forest,' Naia said. 'It was you, wasn't it?'

'Yes, it was me. I came upon that nasty little scene almost too late, and my only thought was to get you away while that oaf was otherwise engaged.'

'Beating Alaric up.'

'Beating me up?' Alaric said.

'I mean Ric.'

'If you'd seen me there,' AU went on, 'the

281

fisticuffs would have finished long before you'd got through interrogating me. So I just ran you out.'

'Isn't it time you told us why you brought us here?' Alaric asked.

AU sighed. 'I suppose it is. I wish there was something for you to sit on to hear it.'

Naia's mouth went dry. 'That bad, is it?'

'You might not see it as the most brilliant news ever.'

They waited while he considered how best to put it.

'Go on then,' Alaric said impatiently.

Still he hesitated. But finally: I won't be absolutely sure until I run a check, but unless I've made a gross error of interpretation, while we've been standing here chatting something's been happening to your realities.'

A further pause invited the inevitable query. And Aldous Uxenden explained.

13: –

For weeks there'd been little doubt in his mind that Alaric's reality hadn't long to go. All the signs were there, signs which almost always augured swift termination. There being nothing he could do to prevent this, he'd closed his mind to it: it was, after all, just one reality among many. But then Alaric had picked up the pouch Naia dropped and come to R43, where AU had answered most of his questions. He'd answered them because once he'd discovered where the boy was from it didn't matter how much he knew. It had been good to talk about those things. So rare to have the opportunity.

What he had not guessed until this very morning was that Alaric's might not be the only reality in trouble. Perhaps it had come to him in his sleep, he had no way of telling; all he knew was that as he emerged from slumber his mind was so burdened with this worry that within half-an-hour he'd left his lodgings above the Sorry Fiddler for the Withern Rise he would soon own, and there, by way of the crossing point under the willow in the north garden, had entered, in quick succession, every reality of his cluster. They were all similar, of course – R43 had been the sole exception – but only that Alaric's and that Naia's had suffered the devastating storm of the night before. Only in theirs had the old oak lost a limb. Only in theirs was there an air of dark expectancy; of fragility. And only their two skies were overcast today, with a red smear that spread as you watched like the blood of a fresh wound through the fibres of a bandage. He'd witnessed such a combination of factors on three occasions over the years, and on each they'd been shared, as now, by just two realities.

As all three cases had concluded with the fusion of those two in a matter of hours, he was certain that Alaric's and Naia's realities were no longer merely parallel, but on the verge of integration. They were about to become one.

'But if two realities merge...' Naia said, hearing of this.

'Yes?' said Aldous U.

'Won't there be two of everything? Everyone?'

'If your realities go the way of the others, you'll end up with a kind of pick 'n' mix of the two, except that no one will have a hand in the picking.'

'You'll have to explain that.'

'Well, let's say a man had a leg amputated in one reality but not the other. The person he becomes when the two realities are joined could be a combination of those two versions of himself.'

'One leg one day, two the next?' Alaric said.

'Shut up,' said Naia.

Aldous U flipped open his satchel and took out the pouch that had taken him to Alaric's earlier. 'Our man could be missing a leg in the new reality but have no memory of losing it. This could easily upset the balance of his mind, but one notion he'll never entertain is that he might once have been two individuals. Nor will anyone else. Family, friends, everyone he knows, will have adapted to the new him without being aware of it.'

'But won't they have any memory of where his leg went?'

'Some might, but probably not all. There'll be a lot of confusion.' He put the pouch in his pocket. 'I'll see if it's happened yet. Don't go away.'

He took a rather theatrical step backward and disappeared. They stared first at the empty space, then at one another.

'Doesn't sound too good for one of us,' Naia said, and walked off, feeling her way step by step as though across treacherous ice. Alaric sank to the 'ground' and folded his legs at the knee.

AU was back in minutes. 'Try the other one now,' he said, exchanging the empty sample-bottle for the fawn-coloured pouch he'd previously used to get to Naia's. 'I might have gone there direct, but it could be risky in the present circumstances.'

Again he took the vanishing step. Alaric and Naia glanced at one another across the expanse, but said nothing.

The next time he appeared, Aldous U said, with a note of triumph: 'Carrying a single pouch, I can see both realities at once from either one. They're a hairline out of alignment, a touch less opaque than normal, but they look the same to the last leaf, twig, blade of grass. And there are two Kates, working at the same task.'

'So what do we do?' Naia asked, heading back. 'Wait for them to merge properly?'

'I think they've already merged. But for them to appear as a single entity we have to treat them as such.'

'How do we do that?'

He took out the pouches that had conveyed him to R39 and R47.

'By using these at one and the same time instead of separately as I've just done.'

'What if you're wrong and they haven't fully merged?' Alaric asked.

'Then we have some waiting to do. Or some rethinking.'

'You said that if there were any differences in the two realities before they were joined only some of those differences would survive. Where does that leave us? I mean…'

He looked at Naia. She understood.

'We won't merge, will we?' she said in alarm. 'Become one person?'

AU shook his head. 'You weren't at home during fusion. That's why I removed you, so it wouldn't happen.'

'But it would have if you hadn't got us out in time?'

'Bet your boots.' He put a pouch in each of his two side pockets. 'And if your next question's going to be would the merged version have been a Naia or an Alaric, I really couldn't say.'

'But personality-wise, memory-wise?'

'Bits and pieces from each of you, is my guess. Prescription for an awful lot of mood-swings, to say nothing of identity crises. Of course, if the physical result had been male,' he added with a grin, 'he wouldn't have had far to look for his feminine side. Shall we go?'

'Go?'

He took Naia's arm, linked it through his.

'I could go alone again, but I'm not sure it would accomplish much.'

'What do you expect to accomplish?'

Instead of replying, he crooked his other arm at Alaric, who said 'I feel stupid' but linked anyway.

'Wait,' Naia said. 'You didn't say what this place is.'

'Did I not?' said Aldous U. 'Oh well. Get ready to breathe now.'

'Breathe?'

He stepped forward, taking them with him, and next thing they knew they were gulping air by the trunk of the willow in the north garden. They were still recovering as AU, more used to this, peered out through the curtain of leaves.

'Well, it *looks* normal…'

They joined him, also peered. The sky was a fine, clear blue and the red blemish was no more, while the garden was in the same post-storm disorder that they'd last seen it, with Kate stooping on the driveway, gathering the last of the broken twigs and tossing them into the old wooden wheelbarrow.

'Dad put an axe through that wheelbarrow ages ago,' Alaric said. 'Bought a new one. Heavy-duty plastic, black and yellow.'

'So it's my reality,' Naia said with cautious relief.

'Not entirely,' said Aldous U.

'Not entirely?'

'I mowed your grass the other day.'

This grass hadn't been mowed for at least three weeks. When all that this suggested had sunk in, Naia said: 'As we weren't in our realities when they merged, how do we know either of us has a place here?'

'We don't, yet,' AU replied. 'But if this works out…'

'Yes?'

'Well, let's see.'

They had taken no more than half-a-dozen steps when the air shivered. Naia and Alaric, at one and the same instant, whispered: 'What was that?'

'Well, I *hope*,' AU whispered back, 'that it's the composite reality modifying itself following receipt of new information.'

'New information?' said Naia.

'The two of you.'

14: 39/47

Kate Faraday looked round at the sound of feet shushing through the uncut grass. She straightened up, smiling.

'I wondered where you two'd got to.'

Naia and Alaric looked at one another. Which two?

'Everything all right here?' Kate said, looking at Aldous U but not quite directing the query to him. Naia made a vaguely affirmative-sounding noise in her throat. 'I'm sorry, have we met?' This time directly to AU.

'You don't know him?' Naia asked.

'I don't think so,' Kate said uncertainly.

'Hullo, Mr Knight.'

All heads turned to see an elderly figure dragging a bloated green garden sack around the corner of the house. Aldous Uxenden nodded to Aldous Underwood as he approached.

289

'Morning, Aldous.'

Naia stared at AU. Kate didn't know him but Aldous *did*?

'Pick 'n' mix,' he said softly, reading her mind.

'What shall I do with this?' Aldous asked Kate.

'We'll have to build a bonfire. Leave it here for now.' He stood the sack against the wheelbarrow. 'Is there much more round there?'

'Stacks,' he said cheerfully.

'I'll come and give you a hand,' Kate said as he started back.

'Righty-ho.'

Naia watched him go, thinking how quickly he'd got over the cat. He was just turning the corner when the sack he'd brought fell sideways and half its contents tumbled out. Kate stooped to repack it. Needing to clarify the situation, and the part she was expected to play in it, Naia said, as casually as she could: 'Any thoughts about where to bury Alaric yet?'

'Bury Alaric?' Kate cast a surprised glance at the human being of that name, standing tense and silent beside Aldous U.

'The cat.'

'Cat? What cat?'

After which, Naia was lost for words. AU stepped into the breach.

'I should tell you what I'm doing here,' he said to Kate. 'My father was gardener here way back. I haven't been within these walls since I was very young, and your son and daughter kindly invited me in for a little look. I hope it's all right.'

Kate looked up at him. 'You're very welcome, but they're not my children. They are brother and sister, though. Twins, actually.'

Alaric's gasp was quite audible.

'It must feel strange,' Kate went on, tying the neck of the sack. 'Seeing the place again after all these years, through older eyes.'

Aldous U smiled. 'Much older eyes.'

She stood up. 'We could do with someone like your father now.'

'Fancy a job?' Naia said pointedly.

He cleared his throat. 'Garden of my own to see to. Good to meet you,' he said to Kate.

'And you. Pop in again, any time.'

'We'll see you out,' said Naia.

She nudged Alaric out of his trance and the three of them set off across the north garden, towards the side gate. They were a few paces short of the path that would take them there when Naia looked back and saw Kate heading for the corner of the house to join Aldous. They waited till she'd gone, then swerved, hurried round the hedge, and to the willow.

'Is this what you expected?' Naia asked as they reached it.

'I'm sorry,' AU said. 'Another huge adjustment for you. For both of you. But if I hadn't done this...' Doubt flickered across his face. 'It's all right, isn't it?'

'I don't know.' She turned to Alaric. 'Is it?'

'Ask me in a week,' he said tautly.

'If just one of us had been accepted here,' Naia said, 'what would have happened to the other?'

'To be honest, I'm not sure.' AU took a number thirty-six pouch from his satchel. 'I might have found myself with a lodger in my new home.'

'Your new home,' Alaric said. 'Is it definite now?'

He beamed. 'Yep. My offer's been accepted. I have my proper Withern Rise.'

Naia said, tentatively: 'Is it...mine?'

'Yours?' Uncertain if he'd shared this confidence, AU threw a glance Alaric's way as he answered Naia with, 'No, no, it's not yours. Another one entirely.'

She contented herself with this. 'When will we see you again?'

He looked at her, a little sadly. 'I think it's best if I keep away from now on, don't you?'

'But all the stuff you wanted to tell me. There's so much I— '

'I've told him most of what I would have told you,' he interjected. 'I'm sure he'll fill you in.'

To which she gave a scornful snort. 'Him? He's a teenage boy. The only kind of communication he knows is the grunt.'

'Oh, this'll be *fun*,' Alaric muttered.

'What will you do now?' she asked AU.

He gave a vague shrug. 'Haven't given it much thought. Learn to relax, finally; potter in the garden; get myself a fishing rod; write my memoirs.'

'Your memoirs!'

'Why not? I've kept extensive records in a very large book: a kind of lexicon of the realities I've visited over the decades, with reams of observations and asides. Make quite a read, presented well.'

'I bet,' Naia said. 'You couldn't publish it, though.'

'I could make a novel of it. Bring it out under an assumed name.'

'*Another* name?'

He laughed, and took her hand. Bent over it. Kissed it lightly. 'Dear girl,' he said tenderly. 'Do take care.'

He nodded at Alaric, passed into the willow, and was gone.

They did not move for some time. Thoughts of any substance eluded them. How should they feel? Behave towards one another? Alaric was less prepared for any of this than Naia. She understood what he did not, quite. That their lives had been rewritten in the past few minutes to account for, and allow, their dual existence here. That among their friends there might be one or two they'd never met. They would both be expected to recall things they hadn't said, done, participated in. There would need to be a great deal of bluffing and quick thinking to avoid stares, snide remarks, nudges behind their backs. The difficulties would be many, and each one would have to be faced up to and dealt with as it presented itself.

'We can't stay here forever,' Naia said at last.

'This reality?'

'This spot.'

As they started towards the house, Alaric said: 'The old boy with the rubbish. I've seen him somewhere. Your friend called him Aldous. Another Aldous?'

'This one lives in the garden. Well, he did last time I saw him.'

'He does *what*?'

'Under the other willow. It's a long story.'

'Aren't they all.'

'I'm glad he's here,' she said. 'I'd hate it if he'd disappeared. He's my great-uncle, you know, give or take a reality. *Our* great-uncle.'

'Ours? I don't even know him.'

'Maybe not yet, but from now on we share relatives.'

'This'll take some getting used to.'

'It will,' Naia said as they crossed the lawn. 'I don't want to even think about some of it. I mean what about—' She halted suddenly. 'Oh, my giddy aunt.' He stopped too. 'There is one thing about us being under the same roof...'

'What?'

'The corner bedroom.'

'What about it?'

'What do you think?'

'Well, it's mine. Always has been.'

'Always been mine too.'

'We can't both have it.'

'No. We can't. One of us must be in a different room here. Question is, who?'

'Only one way to find out.'

'Yes.'

They went on, towards the house, but with every step they walked a little faster, until it became a competition. Then they were running like children, fighting to be first through the front door, first along the hall, first up the stairs with a great clatter of feet and much shoving and shouting.

Then they were making a racket all the way along the landing.

They stopped at the closed door of the room in which they'd both woken almost every morning of their lives. Paused there for a count of ten before Alaric gripped the old brass door-knob. Naia closed her hand on his. They turned the handle, slowly.

Entered.

FLASH 5

Muted light behind the blinds of the corner bedroom. A lean figure moving across. Aldous. She liked the thought of him up there, in the room he'd had as a boy and had again now as a young man in that old body. She turned round on the landing stage, to which no boat had been tethered since she was a girl. Dark as it was – Aldous's window the sole source of artificial light – the river glowed faintly between the two great willows that spilled over and draped the water, while the bushes and leaning trees of the far bank were as tangled and dense as ever. Unchanged, all of it, the way she hoped it always would be. Standing beside this treasured stretch of the Great Ouse, amid the musty odours of this clear October night, it might have been 1988, the year she was born, or 1947, the year the place was signed over to strangers – any year in Withern's lengthening history;

a history she was so glad to be part of, whatever the reality; that her child was going to be part of. This thought brought a warm and very tender melancholy worlds away from sorrow; a rich and personal melancholy to be savoured rather than overcome. Savouring it now, beneath a sky brisk with stars, she was unprepared for the sharp kick inside her, or for the feeling that followed it of no longer being alone. Turning her head, she saw herself, with longer hair, differently dressed but equally pregnant, gazing back at her as if to say, 'I feel it too,' referring not to the kick, but to the Withern-induced melancholy. Such sightings were rare these years, but she was no more alarmed or frightened by it than was the other Naia, as they withdrew, in seconds, from one another's worlds.

'Hi, Sis.'

The moment he spoke it was as though she'd known he was coming.

'Hi, Bruv.'

Standard forms of address after some time apart; frivolous, offhand, their own little joke. To everyone else, even his partner Chris, even Kate, they'd always been brother and sister. It hadn't been easy at first, thanks largely to the aggressive insecurities of his late teens; but in the years since, following their independent departures from Withern to take up jobs and liaisons elsewhere, they'd become very close. The old boards creaked as he stepped down onto them.

'Didn't hear you arrive,' she said.

'We gave the car-horn fanfare a miss for once. How's junior?'

Her hands fluttered to the bump. 'Kicking like a bastard.'

'Showing who's boss.'

'Probably. How's Chris?'

'He's good.'

'Forthcoming as ever, I see.'

'What do you want, a blow by blow account?'

'Heaven forbid.'

The fact was that the day Alaric met Chris – coming up to five years ago now – everything had clicked into place for him, and at thirty-one he was as contented as he'd ever hoped to be. There were some things he couldn't talk to Chris about, of course, but whenever he felt a need to rake over that old stuff, or speculate on what-might-have-been, Naia was just a call away, and Withern, which they owned jointly, was always there.

'What the hell have you done to your hair?' he asked.

'The wind took it.'

After this they fell into a companionable silence, side by side within arm's reach above the quiet water. It wasn't, as Kate surmised, the talking time they needed when together, but to be with the one person who knew their mind, and how they'd become who they were. Only when they were together at Withern Rise did they feel truly complete. As one.

'I'd say there's nowhere like it,' Alaric said after a while, echoing her own thought, 'but it wouldn't be true.'

'Wouldn't be remotely true,' she whispered. 'But this one'll do me.'

'For good?'

'For good, now.'

Some minutes later, they ascended the steps and the grassy slope to the house. At the back porch, left unlit by each of them in turn, one of them said: 'Back to reality.' When they went in, Kate and Chris asked what was so funny. They never did find out.

EPILOGUE

During the ten years following Naia's return to Withern Rise, a great deal of construction work took place in the area.

An extensive house-building programme so reshaped the landscape around Eynesford and Stone that by the end of that time the countryside was no longer a mere stroll away. Most of the buildings along one side of the village street were bought up and demolished in order for the road to be widened and, in part, transformed into a cobbled piazza dotted with young trees, benches, restaurants and shops. The church was sold and its interior rearranged to accommodate several small businesses, including a home-letting agency, a multisex 'hair & body salon', and an ersatz gothic café tragically called The Priest's Hole.

The Coneygeare, already reduced in size by a succession of district councils who saw no point to it, finally lost its common-land status to fifty-five two-bedroom starter homes. The name was retained for the new estate, but few of the children or their starter parents knew or cared that the land on which they lived, played and watched hundreds of TV channels had, until recently, been a meadow for free public use since the fourteenth century, when an equally disremembered king decreed it so.

Nor did Withern Rise escape the cavalier scamper of time. A compulsory purchase order forced the sale of most of the north garden and the loss of access from the side gate. The primary school was closed, the lane turned into a road, and pallid blocks with green roofs soon covered all the land between the former woodyard tributary and the garage in which Naia and Kate parked their small Honda. A brick wall was erected to separate the diminished Underwood See from The Eynesford Project, but as the statutory height limit was two metres, much of the remaining garden became the view from some two dozen back bedroom windows.

Aldous Underwood passed away in his sleep after almost thirty-seven years of active life. The death certificate recorded his age as ninety-six. His great-

great nephew took over the corner bedroom, and was happy to do so, for the two had been close in a quiet sort of way. That was four years ago. Alexander Aldous Underwood (who likes to be called Lex) is now fifteen, Kate is sixty-seven, and Naia three-and-a-half years shy of fifty.

On a certain night in April, Lex wakes from some forgettable dream and can't get back to sleep. After half-an-hour's tossing and turning, he gets up and goes to the window that overlooks the river. If there's a moon it's in hiding, but the exterior lamps of the 'luxury riverside condos' on the opposite bank provide all the light the casual watcher could need. Lex can just remember what it was like to look out and see nothing but a confusion of trees and bushes over there. It's not a view he misses. He likes the balconied dwellings with their shared courtyards and docking points, the line of small craft bobbing at the water's edge – and the windows, many of which are lit up at night, supply considerable titillation through the old binoculars bequeathed to him by the room's previous occupant.

The view from his other window is less thrilling. Nothing to see from there but the cornucopia of trees and shrubs planted by Kate and his mother in a determined effort to make something of the south garden after decades of bland lawn, the sole reminder of whose day is the stump of ancient oak that he and friends from The Coneygeare Estate and the Project used to jump from, yelling, when they were younger.

Wide awake now, Lex pulls on his dressing gown and goes downstairs. He descends in darkness, knowing the stairs too well to need the way illuminated. With no thought as to where he might go on reaching the lower hall, he opts for the River Room, it being just a couple of strides away. He turns the lights on, but once the door closes behind him he is stuck for distraction. Some magazines and papers that don't interest him, pictures on the walls that he knows too well, nothing else. He envies his friends in their modern homes, entertainment points and facilities in every room. Here, just walls, books, ornaments, history. He decided recently that when he's older, when Mum and Kate and his uncle are gone and the place is his, he'll sell up. There are a lot of sentimentalists with more euros than sense who'll pay fortunes for rambling old dumps like Withern Rise. Or maybe he'll flog it to developers, who'll demolish it and put up housing of *this* age in its place.

He stands for a while at the French windows, but with the lights on all he can see is his own reflection.

When interest in the way he looks in dark glass wanes, he turns away, thinking he might as well go back to bed. But as he turns, his eye falls on his mother's latest wall-hanging. Used to these things, he wouldn't ordinarily waste a glance on them, but this one's new, to him as well as the room, and one of her best. He goes to it, runs a hand through it.

Naia's wall-hangings are not pretty by any standards, or very colourful – she dislikes overtly attractive artefacts and has a fondness for earth colours and what she calls 'seasonal tones'. In spite of this, or because of it, demand for them is growing, though she never advertises. They're not orderly, these things; they're uncouth, they intrude, they're hard to ignore. The largest of them, like the present one, measures about a metre-and-a-half from top to bottom, and stands out from the wall by five centimetres here, twenty there. No two are alike, but all are made of similar materials – coarse string and rope, tangled wool, fragments of rag and lace – which she dyes or distresses before tying or knotting selections together in a fairly balanced assemblage. To these she fixes feathers, frayed ribbons, old beads, and small pieces of wood carved into elementary forms that please her. The wooden appendages to this latest offering come from an old spruce, to which she recently macheted her way through the strip of jungle along the periphery wall of the south garden.

Lex pretends disdain for his mother's work, but secretly admires her for creating such idiosyncratic articles. His hand is fondling one of the small pieces of spruce when a sharp pain slithers up his arm and bursts in his chest. He yelps and stumbles backwards, but instead of crashing into furniture continues to fall – dimly aware that the ceiling and walls have given way to dark trunks and branches – onto something brittle that splinters and springs up around him. Raising a hand to protect his face, he feels, fleetingly, empty space beneath him; but then he's back in the room, half-sitting, half-lying on the carpet, and there's a ceiling again, and walls. The pain has already abated, but even if it hadn't it might not be his point of focus now, for the door is opening. He looks towards it, expecting Kate or his mother, but someone else comes in, a girl he's never seen before – in a dressing gown, as though she lives here.

Alexandra Ivana Underwood (who insists on being called Ali) stiffens at the sight of this unknown boy, this total stranger, sprawling on her floor.

'Who are you?' she demands. 'What are you doing in our house?'

WHO BELONGS TO WHICH REALITY

R36. Naia's original reality, which became Alaric's at the end of *A Crack in the Line*. There's no Aldous here, but Mr Knight is Alex's confidant.

R39. The Naia who lost her mother to the Alaric of Reality thirty-six now lives here with his father and Kate Faraday. Old Aldous has taken up residence under the willow tree by the south garden. Mr Knight is prominent here.

R43. The gloomy, dying reality where Aldous U has lived for seven years.

R47. Alaric lives here with his father and Kate. There's no Aldous, no Mr Knight. This Alaric hasn't seen Naia, or visited another reality, since February.

R78. The reality with the Alsatian and fallen fences, where Underwoods have not lived since 1924.

R82. The reality in which Aldous U, searching for news of missing boys, takes a break at the Baker's Oven opposite Stone market square before going on to the seventh and last reality of the day.

R114. A reality from which, in July, an Alaric was transferred to Reality forty-three, where he became known as Ric.

About the Author

In **The Aldous Lexicon**, Michael Lawrence explores the twin themes of Chance and What-might-have-been that have preoccupied him since his teens. The setting for the trilogy is Withern Rise, a substantial riverside property closely based on his grandparents' house, where he himself saw the first light of day in another reality. His bedroom, in an upper corner of that house, is the room that Alaric and Naia Underwood occupy.

You can find out more about Michael on his website: www.wordybug.com

PARTS ONE AND TWO
OF THE ALDOUS LEXICON
MICHAEL LAWRENCE

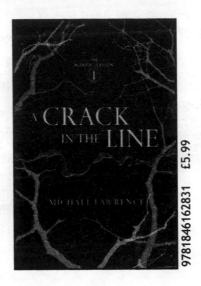

£5.99

9781846162831

'The complexity of the storyline is not something that many
authors could successfully handle; however, Lawrence
has written with a truly cunning hand.'
Independent on Sunday

THE
ALDOUS LEXICON
2

SMALL
ETERNITIES

MICHAEL LAWRENCE

£5.99

9781843628705

'Michael Lawrence's trilogy is a spine-tingling thriller about parallel
worlds. In the first, *A Crack in the Line*, a bereaved boy, Alaric,
steps into the way his world would be had his mother not died.
The difference is, he's a girl. In *Small Eternities*, Naia, his identical
'twin' finds out she's not the only traveller. These are brilliant,
thought-provoking novels…about grief, responsibility and choice.'
The Times

MICHAEL LAWRENCE

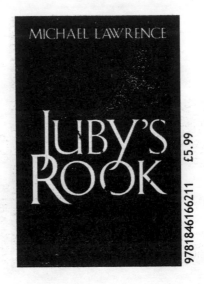

£5.99

9781846166211

Seized and evacuated by the War Office in 1943, the village of Rouklye has been in ruins for decades. When the decidedly odd Juby Bench shows fifteen-year-old Midge Miller round the ruins, she is intrigued. Her interest is further heightened by the appearance of the 'almost-there boy', whom she takes for the ghost of Juby when he was a lad. But how he be, when Juby is still alive, all these years later...?

BERNARD ASHLEY

£4.99

9781843626497

When Ben Maddox is thrust into an investigation for Zephon TV, he worries that he's in over his head. But as he digs deeper into events, he realises that what's really important is being prepared to fight for what you believe in...and if that means taking risks, then that's exactly what he'll have to do.

'*Ten Days to Zero* is a brilliantly constructed thriller...Hopping through various formats, the reader is drawn into a narrative web that is utterly absorbing.'
The Guardian

BERNARD ASHLEY

£5.99

9781846160592

Ben Maddox is sent to find out what's really going on in Kutuliza, in Africa, and finds himself face-to-face with slick politicians, guerrilla fighters and a young boy who is the hope of football and his people. The situation is explosive – and Ben puts everything on the line...

'A powerful and exciting thriller'
Carousel

BERNARD ASHLEY

a BEN MADDOX assignment

FLASHPOINT

BERNARD ASHLEY

9781846160608   £5.99

Ben Maddox is in trouble. After disobeying orders on his last assignment, Ben has been banished by his boss to work in the archives at Zephon TV. But he is desperate to follow up on a hot lead he has received about a drug-trafficking gang. To Ben's dismay, when his boss eventually relents, she give him the show-biz brief – but it turns out to be much more dangerous than Ben could ever have imagined...

BRIAN KEANEY

On the island of Tarnagar is an asylum where you can be locked up
for dreaming. Dante works in the kitchen and Bea is the privileged
daughter of doctors. When their worlds collide, they are forced to
confront the extraordinary evil lurking behind Dr Sigmundus,
the ruler of their nation.

'A remarkable piece of writing, broodingly atmospheric'
The Times

'This gripping thriller has the freshness and philosophical drive of
Philip Pullman's *His Dark Materials* with a substitution of spirituality
and belief for that of inspiration and creativity.
A must-read for all creative, free thinkers.'
Book for Keeps

BRIAN KEANEY

9781846160875 £10.99

9781846160899 £5.99

Avaliable May 2008

Dante is on the run, Bea is in prison and Ezekiel is wounded.
Things do not look good for Púca, the tiny band of indivdudals
who refuse to accept the authority of Dr Sigmundus.

And they're about to get a whole lot worse.

In the depths of the Odyll a new kind of evil is about to be born.
Its name is Gallowglass and its mission is simple. Hunt down and
destroy those who will not obey. Only Dante can stop it. To do so
he must face a terrible choice and discover the dark secret at the
heart of his own family.

The Gallowglass is the second book in *The Promises of Dr
Sigmundus* trilogy, continuing the thrilling journey that began in
The Hollow People.

ORCHARD BOOKS YOU MAY ENJOY